I0779557

STEALTH GENESIS

VIKKI KESTELL

A NANOSTEALTH PREQUEL

BONUS CONTENT
The Christian and The Vampire

Faith-Filled Fiction™

www.faith-filledfiction.com | www.vikkikestell.com

STEALTH GENESIS
A Nanostealth Prequel
With Bonus Content: *The Christian and The Vampire—A Short Story*

BOOKS BY VIKKI KESTELL

NANOSTEALTH

Book 1: *Stealthy Steps*
Book 2: *Stealth Power*
Book 3: *Stealth Retribution*
Book 4: *Deep State Stealth*, 2019 Selah Award Winner
Book 5: *Stealth Insurgence*
Book 6: *Stealth Triumph*
Stealth Genesis, A Nanostealth Prequel

A PRAIRIE HERITAGE

Book 1: *A Rose Blooms Twice*
Book 2: *Wild Heart on the Prairie*
Book 3: *Joy on This Mountain*
Book 4: *The Captive Within*
Book 5: *Stolen*
Book 6: *Lost Are Found*
Book 7: *All God's Promises*
Book 8: *The Heart of Joy—A Short Story*
Book 9: *Rose of RiverBend*

THE TAHOE MYSTERIES

Book 1: *Number 1 with a Bullet*
Book 2: *Be Quick or be Dead*
Book 3: *Death on the Big Blue*
Murder by Accident,
—A Miss Finch Prequel

GIRLS FROM THE MOUNTAIN

Book 1: *Tabitha*
Book 2: *Tory*
Book 3: *Sarah Redeemed*

LAYNIE PORTLAND

Book 1: *Laynie Portland, Spy Rising*
Book 2: *Laynie Portland, Retired Spy*
Book 3: *Laynie Portland, Renegade Spy*
Book 4: *Laynie Portland, Spy Resurrected*
Book 5: *Vyper, A Laynie Portland Sequel*

STAND-ALONE BOOKS

I Can't Hear You,
—A Christian Psychological Thriller
The Christian and the Vampire,
—A Short Story

STEALTH GENESIS WITH BONUS CONTENT,
THE CHRISTIAN AND THE VAMPIRE—A SHORT STORY

Copyright ©2022 Vikki Kestell
ISBN: 978-1-970120-46-2

STEALTH GENESIS
A Nanostealth Prequel
Vikki Kestell

Stealth Genesis and *The Christian and the Vampire*
are available individually in eBook format

"GENESIS" MEANS ORIGIN OR BEGINNING. Stealth Genesis, the prequel
to Stealthy Steps and its award-winning series, Nanostealth, reveals
the never-before-told backstory of Dr. Daniel Bickel. Bickel, world-
renowned nanophysicist, and his devoted technicians, Rick and Tony,
explore the tunnels of the old Manzano Weapons Storage Facility and
brave the danger of discovery in order to locate a forgotten Cold War
devolution site—a cavern carved deep within the mountain to be used
as a presidential command center in the event of nuclear war.

Forgotten by most, *two* such caverns were carved out of the
mountain's rock. While the location of the first devolution site is known,
the *second* cavern, situated far deeper than the first, was intended as a
secret fallback position should events of war require it. This second site
was so highly classified that knowledge of its existence has all but
perished over time, as those charged with its secrecy died and carried
their knowledge to the grave. Dr. Bickel has spent more than a decade
seeking and obtaining documentation and schematics that would prove
the second cavern's existence and, eventually, lead to its location.

When Bickel and his team at last locate and gain entrance to the
cavern, they establish a hiding place for Bickel and his greatest achieve-
ment: a cloud of "smart" nano devices—a swarm *trillions strong*—able
to learn and adapt to new circumstances. Bickel calls these submicron
devices *nanomites*. He predicts his technology will eventually eradicate
diseases, correct birth defects *in utero*, and rid the world of the pests that
destroy crops. Within the safety of the mountain, Bickel studies and
teaches the nanomites, intent on preparing them for their triumphant
public reveal. Bickel will succeed only if he can evade a black-ops branch
of military intelligence bent on seizing the nanomites.

Ambition-driven Air Force Brigadier General Imogene Cushing
has dogged Bickel's career for decades seeking the right moment to
appropriate the nanomites for "national security" purposes. She is the
woman with whom Bickel, thirty-some years prior, shared his first love
affair—the same woman who subsequently absconded with Bickel's
paper outlining his vision of the nanomites and, by her duplicitousness,
irrevocably doomed their relationship.

Scripture Quotations

King James Version (KJV)
Public Domain.

⌘

New International Version (NIV)
The HOLY BIBLE,
NEW INTERNATIONAL VERSION®.
Copyright ©1973, 1978, 1984
International Bible Society.
Used by permission of Zondervan.
All rights reserved.

⌘

New King James Version® (NKJV)
Copyright ©1982 by Thomas Nelson.
Used by permission. All rights reserved.

⌘

Holy Bible, **New Living Translation (NLT)**
Copyright © 1996, 2004, 2015
Tyndale House Foundation.
Used by permission. All rights reserved.

⌘

Cover Design

Vikki Kestell

⌘

DEDICATION

Dedicated to my beloved husband, **Conrad Smith**, who, from the beginning of this series to its conclusion, has been my steadfast support. I could not have completed this important work without you.

⌘

ACKNOWLEDGEMENTS

All my thanks to **Cheryl Adkins** and **Greg McCann**, my faithful proofreaders and fact-checkers. I am honored to work with such dedicated and talented followers of Christ. Our gestalt is powerful!

⌘

TERMS

DEVOLUTION SITE: A remote command center removed from Washington, DC, in time of war to ensure the safety of the President and the continuity of government.

MEMS: Microelectromechanical systems. The field of paired or inter-connected mechanical devices powered by electricity and built at micron or submicron size. (**AMEMS:** Advanced microelectromechanical systems.)

SANDIA NATIONAL LABORATORIES: One of three National Nuclear Security Administration research and development laboratories in the United States. Headquartered on Kirtland Air Force Base in Albuquerque, New Mexico, Sandia's primary mission is to develop, engineer, and test the nonnuclear components of nuclear weapons and technology.

⌘

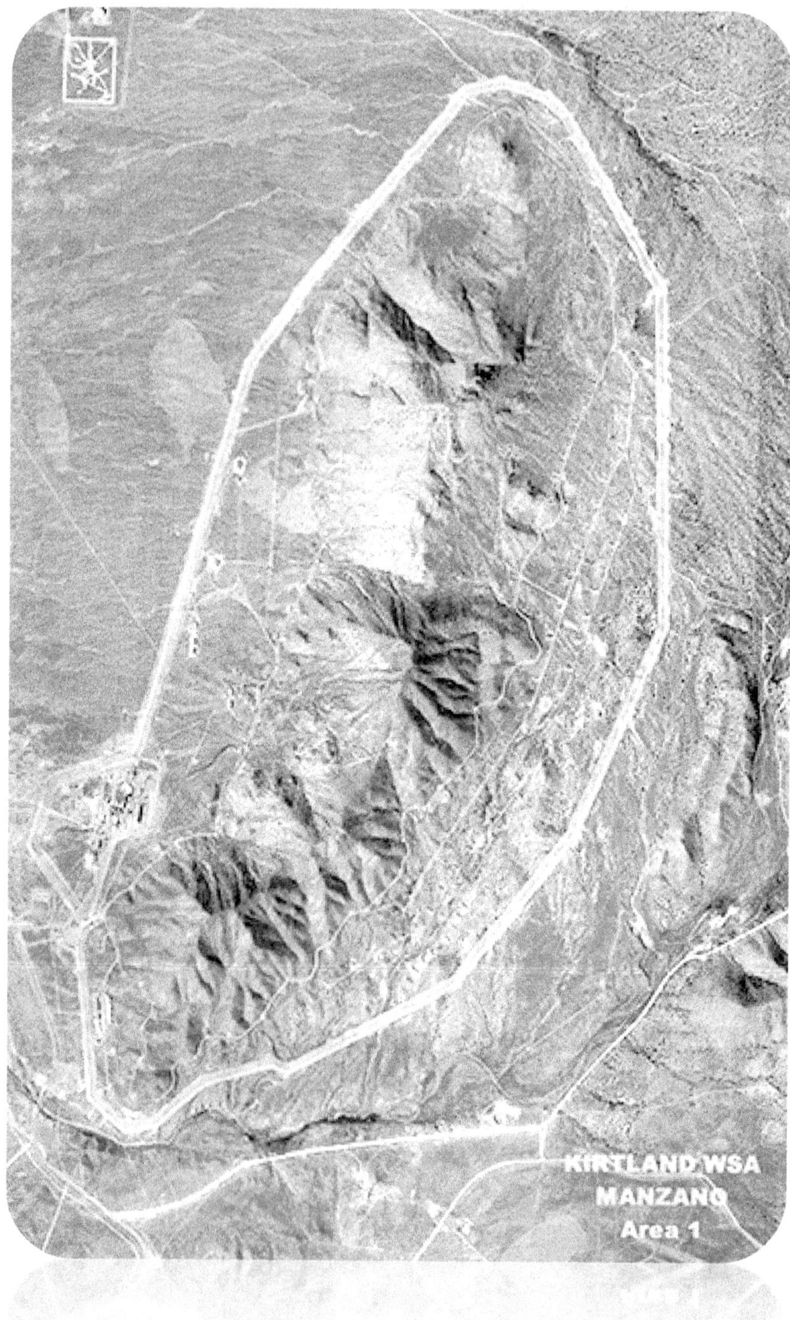

Figure 1. Manzano Weapons Storage Area, Google Earth 2008. Retrieved January 27, 2015, from The Living Moon.

FOREWORD

AFTER WORLD WAR II, at the onset of the nuclear arms race, the US Armed Forces Special Weapons Command constructed an underground facility in the foothills of the Manzano Mountains on what is presently Kirtland Air Force Base, on the southern end of the city of Albuquerque. The site became known as the **Manzano Weapons Storage Facility**.

Hewn into the mountain were four research plants, multiple warehouses, and miles of tunnels—many large enough to drive trucks through. For a time, a large part of America's nuclear stockpile was stored in reinforced concrete and steel bunkers within the mountain.

The facility had other intended uses: During the Eisenhower administration, the military built a devolution site deep inside the mountain—an emergency relocation center. The devolution site was designed to serve as a remote command post for the President and his staff in the event of nuclear attack.

To protect the complex, the military built one hundred twenty-two magazine bunkers around and into the foot of the mountain. Forty-one of those magazines provided direct entrance to the facility via tunnels, and armed forces guarded the mountain.

A Perimeter Intrusion Detection and Assessment System (PIDAS) surrounded the mountain. The PIDAS consisted of two tall, razor-wire-topped fences, one electrified, and an alarmed intrusion zone between the fences—a network of sensors buried in the soil to detect the weight of footfalls.

That was during the Cold War. Today is quite different: Weapons are no longer stored in the mountain. Although several bunkers have been repurposed, most of the facility sits empty and unused. The PIDAS and its intrusion zone are no longer active.

With America's nuclear arsenal stored elsewhere, the many mysteries of the mountain remain largely unknown.

To most people.

⌘⌘⌘⌘

PART 1:
AN UNFAVORABLE BEGINNING

Chapter 1

Mid-May

Sandia National Laboratories,
Kirtland Air Force Base,
Albuquerque, New Mexico

DR. PETREL PROCHANSKI cleared his throat to quiet his staff. When he had their attention, he said, "Ladies and gentlemen, please meet our department's newest senior scientist, Dr. Daniel Bickel."

That was the extent of Prochanski's welcome. Although Sandia's federal oversight and contractor leadership had announced Dr. Bickel's imminent arrival and hailed his stature in the scientific community with a great deal of fanfare, Prochanski made no mention of Bickel's many accomplishments. He said nothing to salute the man acknowledged as the world's foremost authority in nanotechnology and microelectron-mechanical systems, a pairing touted as "nanophysics."

Prochanski, a physically robust man with an overbearing personality (and the ego to match), preferred to be the star in any setting. He most certainly did *not* wish his status upstaged by Bickel's fame and reputation or the man's personal wealth. While Prochanski had lobbied for the labs to hire Bickel, he had not reckoned that the man's stature might overshadow his own standing as department head—or that Bickel's ego might be larger than his own.

Exponentially larger.

The two had clashed the moment Bickel set foot in Prochanski's office. Prochanski's rejoinder was to downplay Bickel's welcome. In Prochanski's mind, the fact that the newcomer cut a rather under-whelming figure mildly mitigated the situation.

Bickel, in his mid-fifties, possessed spindly legs, a slight potbelly, thinning, rust-colored hair, and scraggly brows and beard of the same shade. In any setting, Prochanski's vigorous physique dwarfed Bickel.

Prochanski even "forgot" to announce the addition of two technicians to his staff, men who had assisted Bickel in his work for the past decade or longer. Nevertheless, the department's ovation was enthusiastic—too enthusiastic for Prochanski's liking.

He lifted his hand and called for quiet, cutting short his staff's applause. "Do make Dr. Bickel feel at home, but bear in mind that we have a demanding schedule ahead of us. Fifteen minutes should suffice. Thank you—that is all."

Prochanski strode from the conference room, leaving Bickel and the other fifteen staff members to make small talk over muffins and coffee.

Into the lull, Bickel spoke his first words, "I'm certain it wasn't an intentional oversight, but as I am not the only new staff member, please let me introduce Rick Johnson and Tony Fortuna, my loyal technicians."

The applause this time was longer. When it ended, staff members approached to shake hands, offer names, and utter words of welcome, after which most of the personnel grabbed a muffin and a cup of coffee and left the conference room.

Last in line to greet Bickel and his techs was a soft-spoken young woman. "Hi. I'm Gemma, the department admin. See me for office supplies or anything else you need? Oh. And I'll provide you with your orientation schedules."

"Thank you," Rick said. Tony echoed him.

With her departure, the conference room stood empty except for Bickel and his techs.

Rick smirked at Bickel. "Gee, Doc, wasn't *that* the most enthusiastic welcome ever? I tell ya, I'm overcome."

Tony laughed. "I've received pink slips more graciously worded than Prochanski's little speech."

"Little is right," Rick said. "He hates you already, Boss."

Bickel huffed. "Prochanski is accustomed to top-dog status and the limelight that comes with it. More power to him—if it keeps the focus off of *us*. You both know how circumspect we must be to keep our progress under wraps, how close we are to achieving our goals.

Rick, what's the status of our equipment? How long before we're up and running?"

Rick looked to Tony as he answered. "A week for the installs, another to complete tests and calibrations?"

"Agreed," Tony said.

"Good. We cannot afford to lose even two weeks, but we'll muddle through this settling-in phase and somehow make up the lost time. As for interactions with the rest of the department staff? Keep them to a minimum, and let me handle Prochanski. If that blowhard asks you anything? Refer him to me."

"You got it, Dr. B," Tony murmured.

"In the meantime, as soon as I acquire network privileges, I'll download a bogus set of my data onto the department's node. I'll create a hidden partition, download my real data to it, and move ahead with modeling our latest nano devices."

He paused and stroked his chin hairs. "By the way, I've come up with a name for them, something to set them apart from our older, single-function nanobots. I've given them a name with appropriate distinction. I call them *nanomites*."

Rick grinned. "Nanomites! I like it."

"Yeah, well I'm stuck on what you said before that," Tony said. "You don't think Sandia IT will catch on to your hidden partition?"

Bickel chuckled. "Them catch on to me? Not a chance. Come on. Let's get started."

He exited the conference room, Rick and Tony behind him, but stopped short—startled to nearly collide with the department's administrative assistant mere feet beyond the doorway.

Not quite making eye contact, she held out three sheets of paper. "I have printed the orientation schedule for you and your team, Dr. Bickel."

He studied her detached expression. "It's Gemma, yes?"

"Yes, sir."

"Thank you, Gemma."

"You're welcome, Dr. Bickel."

Bickel ran an assessing eye over her as she turned away. Medium brown hair. Medium height and build. Nondescript features. Ordinary, really. Nothing that would stand out in a crowd.

Nothing to incite concern.

Except that she had been standing less than three feet from him and his team as he expressed his low opinion of Prochanski and they discussed the urgency of their work.

Not to mention my intention to set up a hidden partition on the department node.

How much did she hear?

He said quietly, "Rick? Tony? Don't get into the habit of speaking directly to that girl. If you need something, use email."

"Her? Rather a dull sort, if you ask me."

"Never forget that she's Prochanski's admin. Watch yourself around her."

⌘⌘⌘⌘

CHAPTER 2

SIX MONTHS LATER

BICKEL'S SCOWL COULD have curdled milk. "I've got bad news and bad news, boys. The first of the bad news is that Sandia's federal oversight has decided to separate our work from the MEMS program. Our new program will be called AMEMS, *Advanced* Microelectromechanical Systems."

Tony squinted. "That's bad news?"

"Did you miss the part where I said Sandia's *federal oversight?* Our dear Dr. Prochanski has been flapping his flipping jaws *to the feds* who oversee the labs' work. He's been touting our progress to them! We don't want that kind of attention, particularly from the military-industrial complex or from the military intelligence community—an oxymoron if I've ever heard one."

Tony grimaced. "Oh. Right."

"Yes, *right!* I'll never surrender my work to the US military or intelligence machines, but we're in no position to cut and run at this juncture. The single upside to today's news is that we're moving to a larger lab—and I'll get the money we need to build a 3-D printer to my specifications and equip it with the nanopore print head I designed. The print head hasn't come out right yet, but with additional work, I am certain it will."

Rick sighed. "More space will be welcome but . . ."

"But it comes with more scrutiny," Tony finished.

"You can bet your 401k it does. And can you guess who's moving with us? That pompous windbag, that mediocre excuse of a scientist, *Prochanski*. He thinks he'll be 'directing' and 'overseeing' my work— and yet he can't even follow my briefings! I hear he's bringing Gemma Keyes over, too. Promoting her to part-time project manager."

"Project manager? As in keeping tighter tabs on us?" Rick said.

"No doubt about it. Prochanski informed me that Gemma will collect weekly updates from us—and he's bringing in two postdocs and three more techs to 'assist.'"

Rick considered for a moment. "Hey, you know how we're running dual R&D tracks, feeding Prochanski and the feds 'promising' data? Additional staffing might make running those tracks easier. What if we assign *them* the bogus lines of R&D we've been conducting on the side? We could send them down the rabbit trails while we focus on bringing the real development to fruition."

The rabbit trails Rick spoke of were research paths Bickel and his team had already explored and that had resulted in a series of "dumb" nanobots. Bickel had ultimately rejected that entire line of thinking during his previous university tenure. Here at Sandia, though, he and his techs were running the same experiments "on the side" purely to sidetrack their oversight.

To keep Prochanski from realizing how far along Bickel really was.

"Good idea. Might keep them busy and out of my hair. Meanwhile, Prochanski thinks he has access to my data. He hasn't a clue that I've been shining him on from the get-go, hand-feeding him progress reports I wrote three years ago.

"He's too obtuse to realize that the line of research I'm reporting to him eventually dead-ends with the production of clunky, single-function nanobots instead of 'smart' devices that can learn and adapt."

He paused and ran his fingers through his thin beard. "We can't keep his postdocs focused on that go-nowhere line of R&D forever. Eventually they will reach the same conclusions we did, particularly if either of them are exceptionally bright. A year? Two at most, if we're lucky—and I don't feel lucky at the moment."

His mouth tightened. "We have no choice but to accelerate our plans. All of them."

Rick grimaced. "It's time to implement your exit strategy?"

"Yes, but slowly and carefully. Are you both certain you wish to continue?"

"You mean, are we worried about getting caught?" Tony asked.

"Yes. Do either of you want out?" Bickel asked. His sober gaze shifted between them, and he wondered if, at this point, he would lose either of them . . . or both.

Rick exhaled. "Nope. We already discussed this. I'm with you, Doc."

"Me, too, Dr. B," Tony answered.

Bickel exhaled in relief. "Thank you. I don't wish to—I *cannot*—understate or trivialize the risks the three of us will be taking as we go forward. Nevertheless, when we pull the trigger for my disappearance, I will have done everything possible to provide you with unassailable alibis. As long as you don't crack when they put the screws to you, you'll be fine."

He ground his teeth and added, "Whatever happens, we can't allow Prochanski access to my work, my real work. I have no doubt he's already looking to hawk it to the highest government bidder—not to mention that he'll be trying to claim the credit for *my* breakthroughs at the same time."

"Uh, when do we make our initial foray into the mountain?" Rick asked.

Bickel considered the question. "How about I host a planning session over the weekend, say, Sunday evening?" He brightened. "And how about I fix dinner for the three of us?"

Dr. Bickel loved to entertain; moreover, he was an excellent cook.

"If you're cooking, I'll be there with bells on!" Tony said.

Rick laughed. "Oh, you can count me in, too. Me and my good friend—Mr. Appetite!"

⌘⌘⌘⌘

CHAPTER 3

TONY PATTED HIS STOMACH. "Great meal, Dr. B. Especially liked the fresh roasted peppers, onions, and summer squash."

"Those were awesome," Rick agreed, "but I enjoyed dessert best. Haven't had a slice of honest-to-goodness homemade coconut cream pie in decades, Doc."

Bickel preened under their praise. "Thank you, boys. I do relish cooking for others, and I don't often have opportunity to pull out the stops, so I appreciate your company this evening. But, since we're finished eating, shall we get to work?"

When they had cleared the table and cleaned the kitchen, Bickel brought out a familiar satchel, its leather cracked with age. He removed a number of tubes from the satchel—the kind of tubes used to store and protect architectural drawings, schematics, and blueprints. He donned white cotton gloves before he opened one of the tubes and withdrew a faded map. Rick and Tony also donned gloves and helped unroll the fragile paper and secure its corners with books.

"As you both know, a dear friend of mine, a mentor of sorts, was first to tell me about the mountain—the old Manzano Weapons Storage Facility built during the Cold War. As a military engineer and foreman over essential projects, he told me many tales of what he witnessed and personally worked on. When he passed away, he left me the blueprints and schematics he'd acquired during the build—acquired and managed to keep.

"I spent years and considerable personal means tracking down other surviving members of certain military and civilian engineering and construction crews, the crews that had bored out the tunnels crisscrossing the mountain."

The "mountain" Bickel spoke of wasn't much to phone home about—not as far as mountains go. It boasted no rugged elevations, no jagged, snow-capped peaks. It was more of a crescent-shaped group of rounded, negligible foothills inside the base perimeter fence, and it existed today without much of a public designation.

But when you said "*the* mountain" to the right people? They knew what you meant. Knew it held its fair share of classified and undisclosed mysteries—past and present. And Bickel, Rick, and Tony were determined to unlock a secret within the mountain, a secret held so close, it had all but been forgotten.

"If you'll recall from our initial review of these documents, this overhead view shows the mountain as it was when first completed. The ring of magazine bunkers around the mountain, the security checkpoint, the roads around the flanks of the mountain, and the PIDAS surrounding the entire site appear much the same today as they did when built.

"Present day, the checkpoint is automated—access is by badge swipe—and the PIDAS is no longer active, meaning the ground sensors are disconnected and the outer PIDAS fence is no longer electrified.

"A unknown quantity of perimeter bunkers currently house ongoing classified projects, and while the first presidential devolution site is considered a classified museum—open to those with security clearances and 'need to know'—many sections of the tunnels are relegated to more banal purposes, such as radiological response training. Access to those tunnels is through various bunkers—bunkers with simple keyed locks. You see, getting inside the mountain where we're interested is the easy part, particularly at night."

Rick frowned. "You've said that before, but how do we get through the checkpoint? And which bunker do we use to access the tunnels? There's like, what? a hundred twenty-two bunkers in all? Where do we get keys to unlock the lucky bunker? And whose car will we drive?"

"Yes, I pondered all those questions. Then I hacked Sandia's Fleet Services Department including the automated gates to their lot. Whenever we go into the mountain, we'll commandeer a vehicle under someone else's Sandia ID. We'll remove the car in the evening and return it before morning. That vehicle's plate will be recorded when we pass through the PIDAS checkpoint as will the ID I present.

"We'll park off the road near the bunker we enter. When we do, any base patrol that runs our vehicle's plates will see that the car and its occupants are inside the mountain on approved official business."

"Whose ID will you use? And what about the rest—the right bunker, the right keys, and so on?"

"I have those issues handled, Rick. The less you know of the *how*, the less you'll be able to say should you be interrogated," Bickel said.

Rick shrugged. "I suppose."

"Good. Now, let's talk about the mountain's *two* devolution sites."

Atop the map, Bickel unrolled a second document, one with more lines and markings. "Here we have a scaled version of the tunnels and bunker entrances as of fifty years ago—without either of the presidential devolution sites marked or indicated. What we won't know, before our first foray inside, is how much the interior of the mountain has changed since these schematics and blueprints were drawn up. DOE or DOD may have widened or added on to the tunnels. May have permanently closed off access to others.

"Back to the two devolution sites. Presently, the *primary* command center, while not open to the public, is well known in DOD and DOE circles. It's been left as-is and treated almost like a museum, a snapshot of how the President would have commanded the military had America been attacked during the Cold War.

"On the other hand, the secondary devolution site has 'gone missing.'"

"I don't get it," Rick said. "How does a presidential devolution site go missing?"

"That is an interesting question, Rick. The location and construction of a second site had to have been kept secret, yes? And you know how carefully I've gone about researching the site, the numerous clandestine interviews I've conducted on this subject, yes?"

"Er, yes. You may have mentioned it?"

"Don't be cute. The father of one of my contacts worked during the site's construction phase and was present when those orders came down. She says her father insisted that some high-up but unidentified muckety-muck ordered that the entrances to the second devolution site be covered up. Note that this man told his daughter *entrances*, plural, not *entrance*, singular."

"By 'covered up,' do you mean bricked over? Blasted? Tunnel ceilings dropped?"

"Could be any of those or something shades more creative."

Bickel unrolled a set of blueprints and spread them atop the map. The blueprints were printed on thin, semitransparent paper, old and fragile. With a delicate hand, he slid the prints atop the map until certain landmarks aligned with the tunnel lines beneath.

"These documents are my most prized artifacts from that era," Bickel murmured. "I have made copies, of course, but these are the originals, left to me when their owner, the dear friend I spoke of earlier, passed. What do you see?"

Rick and Tony perused the blueprints. Tony's gloved finger hovered over a line of small print. "This. It reads 'PDS02. Presidential Devolution Site 02?"

"Good. What else is significant at first blush?"

Rick crowded Tony until their heads were touching. "Does this number indicate elevation? If it does, this PDS02 is about two hundred feet lower than the nearest tunnel entrance—the tunnels themselves being carved into the mountain's flanks, somewhat elevated above the mountain's base."

"That's exactly what it is. Wherever we find and start down the route to the second devolution site, we'll descend two hundred feet to reach it. Because it *is* considerably deeper than the first devolution site, it could be that government decision makers intended it initially as a secret fallback position, an ace in the hole."

"Wow," Tony breathed. "We know where inside the mountain the site is. Approximately."

"Still not the hard part, I'm afraid. Locating an access point to the site? That will be the hard part. And it won't be as simple as you think because the designers of the two presidential command centers were in the habit of adding false doors, diversionary tunnels, and boobytraps to confuse and mislead our enemies should ground forces land and breach the mountain.

"We may be forced to navigate and reject false starts and dead ends. We may spend weeks searching before we locate a *real* route that takes us down, into the heart of the mountain, all the way to the lost devolution site."

He gently lifted the blueprint, set it aside, and pointed to the map of the crescent-shaped mountain formation with the tunnel/bunker schematic overlaid on the map. He placed a gloved finger on a bunker on the southeast side of the mountain. "I propose we make our initial entrance into the mountain here."

Where his finger rested, he placed a red "sticky" arrow. Then he slid the semitransparent blueprint back over the schematic. The red arrow was faintly visible through the blueprint.

"From this bunker entrance, we're within three hundred yards, give or take fifty feet, of PDS02 if the devolution site were at the tunnel level. This bunker and its nearest connecting tunnels are as good a place to start our search as any, but . . ."

"But?" Rick asked.

"We have no assurances that we'd be looking in the right place. The entrance to the cavern could start anywhere inside the mountain and descend from there."

Bickel considered his friends. "Let's think about this a minute. We have a lot on our plates at present: Moving to a new lab space. Assigning our arriving postdocs and techs to our old R&D lines while keeping a close eye on what they're doing. Making them think we're following a line parallel to theirs. Presenting their outcomes and our false-but-similar outcomes to Prochanski on a weekly basis. Stringing Prochanski along with hopeful up-and-coming breakthroughs.

"And all that time, we'll be advancing our own R&D, making real inroads, but keeping our results absolutely compartmentalized. I might even 'hide' another set of faux data where Prochanski can find it if he goes sniffing around. If he finds the data, he's less likely to keep looking, right?"

"Right," Rick muttered. "What about the mountain?"

"I suggest, initially, that we make one foray every two weeks. Unless something changes drastically, we have adequate time to locate the route."

"When will we start?" Tony asked.

"How about Wednesday, say 10 p.m.?"

Rick blew out a breath he hadn't realized he'd been holding. "Yeah. Get inside. Get the lay of the land, so to speak."

They didn't discuss further how long it would take them to find an access point that led to the forgotten devolution site . . . or if they ever would.

⌘⌘⌘⌘

CHAPTER 4

WEDNESDAY EVENING

BICKEL RAN A HAND through his thinning rust-colored hair as he peered into the darkness. He checked his watch and used his fingers to comb his beard—purely a nervous gesture.

"It's time," he announced quietly.

He slipped out a door that bypassed the AMEMS' lighted parking lot. Tony followed. Setting a deliberately unhurried pace, they crossed the adjoining street, walked to the corner, and approached a vehicle parked under a tree. The car—a small, nondescript sedan "borrowed" from Sandia's Fleet Services Department—was nearly invisible within the tree's nighttime shadows.

No lights came on when Tony opened the passenger side door and Bickel a rear door. They said nothing as they climbed inside. Immediately, the car's engine started. The driver pulled onto the nearest street. A block away, he switched on the headlights.

Bickel leaned forward, between the two front seats. Even with the windows shut tight and the radio providing low white noise, Bickel didn't speak above a whisper.

"Good job, Rick."

"No sweat, Doc."

"GPS?"

"I used your device to unlock and start the vehicle, then disable the GPS tracking. A handy little piece of tech! We should have the car back to the motor pool before they know it's missing."

"Thanks, Rick." Bickel sat back and allowed himself to breathe. Willed himself to calm.

He trusted Rick and Tony implicitly. They had been his vital teammates during Bickel's tenure at Stanford and later at Georgia Tech. They had followed him to Albuquerque when Sandia hired him. The two men had chosen to relocate with him at these advancements, uprooting their families to remain with him.

And why wouldn't they? As the world's leading authority in nanophysics, Bickel had mastered and expanded the nanotech body of knowledge.

In addition, Bickel owned an impressive computational mind. In fact, Bickel's skills as a hacker would have been legendary had he chosen to make his fame that way, if he had cared to hold such a reputation— which he did not. No, Bickel cared for *the nanomites*, his creation and the culmination of his life's work. He best employed his nimble mind and fingers writing the complex algorithms that framed the nanomites' intelligence, the "smart" technology that allowed them to learn.

Finally, Rick and Tony were more than Dr. Bickel's techs; they were his closest friends. They believed in Bickel's vision. Bickel, in turn, relied upon the two men more than he relied upon any two people on the planet. They had remained his stalwart supporters as Bickel drew closer to his goal, the goal he had labored toward for thirty-five years.

Their unflinching loyalty was why Rick and Tony were part and parcel of the night's stealthy foray. It was also why Bickel didn't want anything to go wrong: He didn't want his friends to pay the price getting caught would exact.

They had planned this, their initial sortie, to minimize said danger: The sky above them was dark, the clock read "late," and they'd be short on sleep when tomorrow's workday rolled around. At the same time, they knew that traffic on the base was generally light this time of night and activities within the mountain's classified bunkers were at their lowest ebb.

That said, they were aware that Air Force security patrols roamed Kirtland day and night. Bickel shifted uncomfortably. Were base police, at this moment, following Bickel and his techs, taking note of their midnight jaunt?

Rick pulled onto 20th Street SE, south of the base's Eubank gate, then turned onto a dirt road, a well-used shortcut, and headed south. He maintained a moderate, unhurried speed. Minutes later, the road intersected with Pennsylvania SE, adjacent to the base's golf course.

In town, Pennsylvania ran due north and south. On the base, the street took about a 45-degree left turn and headed southeast, then dead-ended at the mountain's security checkpoint.

Before he pulled onto Pennsylvania, Rick looked both directions.

"See anything?" Bickel asked from the rear seat.

"Doesn't mean they aren't out there, waiting with their headlights turned off."

"Agreed. However, it would look suspicious if we tarried too long here. It would look worse should we turn around rather than go ahead."

Rick nodded his agreement. He turned left onto Pennsylvania and headed east.

Bickel knew—the three of them knew—that they were approaching one of the diciest parts of the night's task. From here, their choice of routes would be limited: Turn *right* half a mile ahead and travel farther south on the base's *fifty-two thousand* acres where their supposed destination could be one of many. Or, instead of turning right, continue east and turn *left* before the security checkpoint and enter the campus of DOE's National Training Center. Basically without egress, the NTC was a place to turn around. To retreat.

But, if they made neither turn, a single destination remained—straight ahead and through the security checkpoint, where they would pass inside the PIDAS—two tall, razor-wire-topped fences running parallel to each other, surrounding their intended destination.

On the other hand, should they be discovered trespassing where they had no right to be, in possession of a cloned ID card and stolen keys, and carrying what amounted to a burglary kit? Losing their jobs and security clearances would be the least of their worries.

Bickel pursed his lips. *If they're watching us tonight, we're already toast.*

⌘⌘⌘⌘

CHAPTER 5

As Bickel had suggested, he and his techs made incursions into the mountain every two weeks. Working their way through the tunnels nearest the estimated location of the second devolution site, using copies of the old schematics to guide them, they tapped every rock wall and floor, studied tunnel support beams, examined side rooms and empty weapons storage lockers, scrutinized facilities left to disuse, and searched nearby bunkers.

Their searches yielded nothing. They did become more comfortable entering and navigating the tunnels, but their many nights of effort to date had been fruitless . . . until the night they opened a maintenance closet in a side tunnel. The closet was used, apparently, to store janitorial supplies and other sundry items, including shelves stocked with lightbulbs.

Strings of lights up and down the tunnels provided illumination within the mountain. Decades ago during the facility's construction, workers had bolted steel conduits to the stone walls, wired the mountain for electricity, and fastened durable strings of lightbulbs down both sides of every tunnel. The dim lights were always on. The bulbs in the closet, no doubt, were there to replace those that burned out.

Bickel stared at the plans for ten minutes, asking himself what was bugging him, what had, unconsciously, brought him to a standstill. He wondered why he continued to glance from the plans to the closet and back.

I'm tired, he admitted. *Long hours in the lab followed by these merry middle-of-the-night jaunts—even limited to twice monthly—wear on me. I'm not as young as Rick and Tony. Can't shake off the loss of a full night's sleep as easily as they can.*

He sighed, lowered the plans and stared down the empty tunnel to rest his vision. Frowned at the closet, then lifted the plans to his eyes.

"I'm an idiot."

Tony looked up. "You asking for an 'amen,' Dr. B?"

"Very funny. No, but I'd appreciate if you'd check this out and tell me I'm not crazy. Tell me what you see. Or, rather, what you *don't* see."

Rick and Tony joined him.

"Hold this edge of the plans, Tony," Bickel said.

When Tony took hold of the plans, Bickel's finger scribed an invisible circle on the paper. "See it?"

Rick and Tony looked to the tunnel wall, then back to the plans. From the closet, to the plans.

Back to the unlocked closet. A closet *not* on the plans in front of them. A closet with metal back walls and sides. Recessed into the tunnel wall itself.

Rick breathed, "I'll be a monkey's uncle."

⌘

THEY HADN'T WAITED another two weeks to look behind the closet; they returned the following night.

When Bickel and Tony slid into the Sandia vehicle Rick had commandeered, Bickel asked in his low, reedy voice, "Do we have everything we need for this critical step? Are we certain?"

Rick started the engine and answered, "Tony and I went out at noon and got everything. We have crosschecked the list four times."

"Right. Yes. Yet there's no sense going in tonight if our equipment isn't ready to go."

Rick and Tony knew Dr. Bickel well; they understood his ego and flaws inside and out. His shifts from confidence in them to micromanagement did not faze either of them.

Tony replied softly, "No worries, Dr. B. We've got it handled."

Bickel laughed under his breath. "Of course you do. I apologize. Nerves."

When they passed through the mountain's security checkpoint, Rick took the main road that encircled the mountain, then turned right. They drove the winding road around the southern tip of the mountain and started up the mountain's east side. Not long after, they reached their usual bunker entrance. Rick pulled off the road, nosed up to the bunker, and parked.

They got out and each of them shouldered a heavy backpack. Tony and Rick carried between them a large bundle of wide metal panels, bound and padded to muffle their sound should they drop the panels or clumsily bang them on a rock wall.

Dr. Bickel used his key to open the bunker door. Inside the bunker, Rick and Tony leaned the bundle of panels against the bunker's wall, and Tony dropped his pack. He left to reconnoiter the route to the storage closet.

He was back in ten minutes. "All's quiet. Didn't see or hear anyone. No unexpected lights."

"Excellent," Bickel said. "Let's proceed."

The three of them walked in silence from the bunker entrance into its adjoining tunnel. Pausing cautiously at every junction they encountered, they retraced their route to the old maintenance closet.

The "closet" was more like a small room, about eight feet wide by ten feet deep, fitted with a standard 1950's military-grade steel door and lock. For whatever purpose the closet had initially been built, the structure was no longer locked. It stored the janitorial supplies and shelves of fresh lightbulbs they'd taken stock of the night before. The remaining items in the closet were a broom, dustpan, and a short trash can containing shards of broken glass.

When they had first laid eyes on the broom and trash can, Tony had surmised, "Guess the facility guys drop lightbulbs once in a while when changing out the dead ones."

That broom, dustpan, and trash can would come in handy.

Rick and Tony put down the bundle of panels and pulled off their backpacks.

"I have first watch," Rick said.

They had carefully planned each step and their assigned roles. The plan called for one of them to stand watch at the nearest junction while the other two worked.

Although the closet door's lock may not have been used for decades, the first thing Tony did was to clean the lock's internal mechanism and rekey it to the set of keys he pulled from his pocket. If someone were to come investigate the noise of their activities, the watch stander would return to the others, and the three of them would step into the closet, close and lock its door from the inside, and wait for the threat to leave.

Tony and Dr. Bickel lost no time unloading the three backpacks, the most important and bulkiest item being a drill. They hadn't brought a simple, handheld tool for the job ahead, though. No, their drill was an industrial diamond coring model mounted on a large base.

While Tony assembled the base, Bickel laid out a 100-foot heavy-duty extension cord along with other tools and necessary paraphernalia. He ran the extension cord down the tunnel to an outlet affixed to conduit on the stone wall beneath a string of lights. When he returned, he lined the trash can with a thick garbage bag. Then he and Tony donned safety glasses and dust masks.

"Ready?" Bickel asked.

"Ready."

Tony nudged the coring bit close to the center of the back wall of the closet and set the machine in motion. The drill's low whirring grew louder as the bit ground through the closet's metal wall. Almost immediately, it encountered something harder.

"We've hit stone."

"Keep going."

The same type of rock that made tunneling the mountain feasible also facilitated their attempts to bore through it. Hitting stone, however, did not answer the question burning in their minds: Would the drill, within a foot or two, punch through to a forgotten tunnel, a hidden passageway leading to the lost devolution site as their examination of the schematics had led them to hope? Or were they boring deeper into the mountain?

The drill's motor geared down, but it kept making slow, tedious progress. That progress cost them two hours and yielded about eighteen inches. They took a break for water and a snack. Tony and Rick traded places. Rick retracted the bit and checked it for damage. He added another length of extension to the bit, and Bickel used the drill's down time to sweep up tailings and pour them into the trash can's liner.

Rick resumed drilling, going farther into the stone behind the closet. Another slow hour passed. The drill was about twenty-two inches into the rock.

Bickel alternated between despair and anger. He glared mindlessly at the back wall of the storage closet.

I was certain we'd find a passageway here. Possibly a direct entrance.

He stood at the door and scanned the interior of the closet. The back wall was around eight feet in width, and they were boring smack in the middle of it. But the closet was about two feet deeper than it was wide.

What if . . .

"Isn't this closet an odd size? Deeper than wide?"

Rick glanced up. "What? Couldn't hear you."

Bickel gestured to him. "Shut it down."

Rick did. "What's wrong?"

"What's wrong is that we're drilling in the wrong place. The passageway entrance isn't *behind* this closet, it's to the *side!* For our next attempt, reposition the base on the right wall, about six inches from the rear corner."

Rick focused on the spot indicated, his mind working. "Did you say this closet was too deep?"

"That's what I said. I keep wondering: Why is this closet recessed into the tunnel wall in the first place? Did someone build it to precisely fit the niche in this tunnel wall?"

"You're thinking they carved out the wall as the passageway starting point, that they added the closet to hide the passage? That the niche itself is the passageway entrance?"

Bickel nodded. "It's a theory—and if my theory is correct, we should be drilling into either the left or the right wall, not the rear wall."

Rick backed the bit out of the hole and started removing the extension arms. He unclamped and removed the drill's head, and shifted the base to the right wall, less than a foot from the corner. "Here?"

"Yes. Try there."

Rick anchored the base and attached the bit. He started the machine's motor, and the bit moved forward. It went through the wall of the closet quickly, as expected. Then straight into nothingness.

"We're through! I've found open space behind the bit!"

Bickel's smile was taut and devious. "Some bright individual had this 'closet' custom made to fit this niche, then he ordered it pounded into the niche and bolted to the surrounding rock—to hide the passage entrance. Ideally, all we need to do is cut a hole in the side wall of this closet and climb through it."

Rick grinned back. "You got it, Doc."

As Bickel watched, Rick drilled a line of vertical holes three feet high through the side of the closet close to the rear corner and a matching line about twenty-four inches from the first. He drilled then a horizontal line about six inches from the floor of the closet, connecting the two vertical lines.

He had started the horizontal line across the top when Bickel said, "I'll get Tony."

When Tony returned with Bickel, Rick had finished outlining a three-foot-by-two-foot rectangle and was shifting the drill base out the way. Tony picked up a battery-powered grinder and began grinding through the closet's wall, connecting the holes, while Bickel retrieved the extension cord.

Another thirty minutes passed. They removed the piece of closet wall and stared into the darkness beyond it.

"You first, Doc," Rick said, offering him a flashlight. "If it weren't for you, we'd still be drilling straight into the mountain."

Bickel nodded. "All right. But we need to get a move on."

Tony locked the closet door behind them, grabbed up the grinder and an extra battery pack, and the three of them, in turn, climbed through the tight hole.

Bickel stopped immediately. "You two notice what I'm noticing?"

"That this tunnel is wide enough for workers to move supplies in and out?"

"Wide enough to drive a military utility vehicle carrying supplies in and out," Bickel said. "How else could they descend two hundred feet down into the mountain, carve out a cavern, and then furnish it for the President?"

"Guess you're right, Dr. B."

The wide passageway ran straight ahead from the closet several yards, then took a ninety-degree turn left for several more yards before turning right. At that junction, the passage immediately widened and presented them with three choices: straight ahead, right, or left.

"Which way, Doc?"

Bickel investigated the choice of tunnels in turn, left to right, while Rick and Tony waited. The left-hand passage dead-ended about fifteen yards in. The straight-ahead passage made three quick turns before Bickel encountered—and nearly fell into—a deep hole that spanned the width of the tunnel.

"Clever," he muttered, "and quite diabolical."

He returned to the junction and told them what he'd found.

"Our route must be down the right-hand passage," Bickel said. They made a wide, downward-sloping right, then left—repeating the switchbacks three more times—all the while descending, moving deeper into the mountain and encountering other tricks and traps.

"Gettin' dizzy here," Rick complained. "And what's with all the turns back and forth?"

"Those in charge of the President's security designed this tunnel to slow and deter attackers, Rick. We can use their methodology to our advantage, and we can improve upon it: Set boobytraps like that pit back there, add more 'dead ends' and bogus junctions, rig a rockfall or two, and install alarms to let me know I'm about to have company."

"Giving you time to get out?"

"I am betting on it."

Half an hour and more diversionary side tunnels later, they arrived at a steel door—a locked steel door with no handle or keyhole. They searched all around the door, felt every square inch, scrutinized every metal or stone flaw. Found no way to open the door.

"Locked from the inside?" Bickel mused.

"Stand aside!" Tony said with humor. He hefted the grinder and went after the door where he estimated the door handle and lock to be on the other side.

Defeating the lock wasn't as easy a task as they'd hoped. He swapped out batteries and kept at it.

Bickel shook his head. "It's getting too late."

"This is going take more time, Dr. B, along with fresh batteries and grinding blades."

"Right. Let's pack it up for the night. Leave the grinder and most of our tools here and come back tomorrow evening."

"Yeah, I'm beat," Rick moaned.

"We all are," Bickel agreed. They retreated to the closet and set about their preplanned cleanup. Bickel ran out the extension cord a second time. Rick and Tony undid the bundle of wide metal panels.

They leaned the panels side by side across the back and right side of the wall. The metal was—deliberately—a close match to the metal of the closet walls, although significantly thinner.

While Rick held the first panel, Tony grabbed a hand drill from the floor and began inserting screws into it. They paneled across the entire back wall to hide their abortive drilling attempt, then paneled across the side wall to cover up the hole into the tunnel. Regaining access to the tunnel behind the panels would be as simple as removing the screws on two of the panels.

As Rick and Tony installed the panels, Dr. Bickel swept until he'd captured every bit of tailing and grit he saw. Then he plugged in a mini vac and vacuumed for good measure. When he was finished, he retrieved the extension cord and wound it up.

"Looks good," Bickel pronounced.

"We'll need more panels to cover the left side wall so that everything matches," Tony said. "We'll grab them during lunch tomorrow and finish the job tomorrow night."

"Sheesh! And here I'd planned a nice nap instead," Rick joked.

Neither Tony nor Bickel responded. By now, the three of them were running on fumes, Bickel more than Rick or Tony.

They repacked the tools they hadn't left in the passageway into a single backpack, hoisted the bag of debris from the trash can, and headed for the bunker door.

They said nothing until they were safely through the PIDAS checkpoint onto Pennsylvania, and had turned onto the dirt road on their way back to Dr. Bickel's lab. Even then they grinned more than talked.

They were exhausted. And elated.

Finally Bickel chuckled aloud and said, "We've done it, men. By golly, we've done it!"

⌘⌘⌘⌘

CHAPTER 6

THE FOLLOWING NIGHT, Bickel and his techs returned to the mountain. This time, they knew how to get inside the hidden passageway. They understood the task before them to gain entrance to the old devolution site.

Bickel locked the three of them into the supply closet while Rick and Tony removed the panels of fake metal wall over the tunnel entrance. Bickel then led the way through the narrow hole they'd punched into a much wider tunnel. Bickel and his techs were able to bring extra lighting with them this time because some of the tools they had packed in the night before were waiting for them at the locked steel door.

Down, down, down the stone passage wound, turning this way and that, taking them deeper and deeper into the mountain. After what they estimated was two miles coupled with a steep descent, they arrived at the steel barrier across the passageway.

Tony powered up his grinder and addressed the locked door with no small amount of glee.

"I've spent the past twenty hours mentally grinding the lock off of you," he laughed. "Now that we're together again? *Let's dance.*"

While Rick held the light, an enthusiastic Tony got to work.

Rather than stand around fidgeting and doing nothing, Bickel retraced his steps. As he went, he memorized every twist and turn, every false branch of the passageway.

He was already imagining how to repurpose the route, how they might add to its complexities, what other diversions and nasty little surprises they could build into it—after he and his techs found the *real* entrance to the old devolution site . . . because Bickel believed he was standing in a passageway that had been carved into the mountain solely for construction purposes.

"Riddle me this, Bickel," he whispered. "If *this* passageway is the only route down to the President's secret command center, then who locked the door? It only locks from the inside—*ergo,* someone had to have been on the other side to lock it—otherwise, when the President arrived to take up the reins of government in this remote site, who would unlock it for him or her?"

The lone possible answer to the question was another entrance.

"The entrance and route to this particular command center—a *secret* presidential fallback position—had to have been known by an exceptionally short list of individuals . . . for national security purposes."

He turned and started back toward Rick and Tony. "Wherever they placed the starting point of that entrance, they disguised it thoroughly enough that no one with access to the mountain has, even to this day, recognized it *for what it is*—hardly a deduction to encourage our efforts—*but!*"

He raised an imperious finger. "While the route's starting point is camouflaged—for all intents and purposes rendered invisible—and when the President was ensconced within the cavern, wouldn't the route's point of return be clearly marked as the EXIT?"

That single reason was why their ensuing move wouldn't be to explore the devolution site: They needed to enter the site and seek out the *actual* entrance.

He snapped his fingers and hurried toward his crew.

"No more of this tunnel cloak-and-dagger nonsense," he muttered to himself. "When we gain entrance to the devolution site, we will find that exit, marked or not. We will find it and thus acquire a simpler, more suitable access to the command center—my future refuge."

His prodigious mind leapfrogged ahead. "After we learn how to access the route's hidden opening from up top, we'll come back to *this* passageway and modify it. And we'll leave a few—*a very few*—faint clues to hint at it. Why? Because when the time comes and those hunting me manage to track me to this mountain? I wish them to find the clues I have left them, the clues that lead them to the supply closet and this passageway."

He grinned at the lovely utility of his idea. "No matter how they break into this passageway or blast their way into it, somewhere along its route they will encounter my surprises—a plethora of wrong turns, boobytraps, and delaying tactics as they push forward. I will hear them coming and have plenty of time to make my escape."

Bickel was chuckling to himself when he came upon Rick and Tony. The locking mechanism, its edges rendered a hot, smoking red compliments of the grinder, lay on the tunnel floor.

"You've breached the door?" Bickel asked.

Tony radiated victory. "Yup. Been waiting for you a minute or two. Figured you'd want to go first."

"Indeed, indeed! Very thoughtful. Thank you."

Tony, heavily gloved to protect his hands from the hot metal edges, inserted his hand into the hole left by the lock's removal and pulled steadily. "Little heavy," he grunted. He braced one foot on the wide jamb alongside the door and pulled harder.

With a groan, the door moved . . . then swung toward them. Rick caught Tony and kept him from landing on his can when the door gave way.

Their elation was short-lived.

Through the doorway, two yards away, stood yet another door.

"Makes sense," Bickel mused. "Defense in depth. Additional delaying tactics."

"Yeah, well let me at it."

This new door swung away from Bickel and his team, not toward them, and it took Tony two more hours to get the door open. He'd ground through the lock, punched out the remains of the mechanism on the inside, and peered through the hole it left—and spied a thick bar across the door.

Rick took a turn putting his eye close to the hot hole in the door, too. "Hang on. I have an idea, Tony."

Rick pulled out a socket wrench, connected an extension and heavy socket to it, then threaded the socket through the hole in the door. Levered the socket under the bar and tried to lift it.

The bar barely budged.

"Try nudging it to the side," Dr. Bickel suggested.

"Huh. Might work."

The heavy bar moved minutely, but it moved. After ten minutes of hand-cramping nudges, Rick felt the bar quiver as one end lost its purchase on the slot in which it had been seated. The bar fell to the floor beyond, taking the socket from Rick's wrench with it.

With one mighty, sustained push, accompanied by the *scree* of the bar scraping along the floor, the door opened and clanged against a stone wall.

They were inside.

⌘⌘⌘⌘

CHAPTER 7

BICKEL WALKED SLOWLY through the doorway, acutely conscious that his were the first feet in going on seven decades to tread this hallowed place. The passageway beyond the door terminated in an alcove on the left, and the alcove . . . opened into a large cavern.

The three of them, side by side, aimed their flashlights into the cavern, taking in its scope and size. "What do you think? A hundred feet across?" Bickel asked.

"Hundred twenty, I'd think," Rick said, "left to right—would that be east to west?"

"According to my compass, that's correct."

They walked their flashlights upward. The cavern's domed ceiling was twenty-five feet or higher at its zenith. As they moved their lights around the ceiling, they spotted a ledge where the vertical walls of the cavern began to bend and curve upward to form the dome.

"See that?" Bickel pointed to the ledge and a string of bulbs covered in dust. "Same lights as in the tunnels. Has to be a light switch around here somewhere."

Rick frowned. "You don't think there's power down here after all these years, do you? I projected we'd have to run wire into the cavern and pirate juice from the tunnels."

Bickel snorted. "Ha! Back in my day, we made things to endure—no built-in expiration dates." With a grimace he added, "Besides which, my plans rather depend upon a decent power supply. I sincerely hope my confidence in the architects and builders hasn't been misplaced. If we take a gander around, we should find a circuit breaker panel or—"

"What—like this one?" Tony had stepped to the side of the alcove and pulled a panel open. He examined it. "Surprisingly clean. Give it a go?"

"Oh, yes. Absolutely."

One by one, Tony threw over five breaker switches. When he threw the third switch, a hum filled the cavern and a gentle glow lit the line of lights. As the bulbs warmed, the lights brightened—followed by three pops and the tinkle of glass falling on the cavern's stone floor.

"Good thing we know where to get more bulbs, eh?" Rick chuckled.

Tony guffawed. "Think anyone will miss a couple dozen?"

"Hey! Perhaps we can get them to restock?"

Then the three of them were laughing and shouting, giving voice to their celebratory glee.

⌘

DESPITE BICKEL'S DESIRE to locate and map the presidential route to the cavern without delay, they spent an hour wandering the perimeter of the cavern. Its shape, they discovered, was not strictly circular but more of an oblong, its length running north and south. Bickel and his techs had made their entrance on the southeast end of the oblong.

At the north end, what they called the "back" of the cavern, the rock walls were not as smooth as the cavern's other walls. The rear wall was rough with ledges, jagged protrusions, and sharp edges, underscoring their belief that work on the site had been incomplete when the cavern was locked up and forgotten.

Office furnishings—desks, chairs, tables, file cabinets, circa 1950— languished across the cavern in no particular order or fashion. The dust of years coated the old furniture.

"We have our work cut out for us, boys, but we're here. We're really here."

"I'm already cataloging what they left behind that's usable and making a list of what we need, Doc," Rick replied.

Bickel wandered over to the right side of the cavern, intrigued by an arched stone doorway. He peered inside and smiled. "Hey, guys? Take a look at this."

The doorway led to two rooms carved from stone, one a kitchen of sorts boasting an old sink with running water. The second "room" featured a long niche carved into the left-hand wall forming a platform that looked suspiciously like a bed. To the right of the room's doorway, they found a tiny stall and a gravity-fed toilet.

"Presidential living quarters?" Tony wondered aloud. "Man, I am *not* impressed."

Rick thought before he answered. "They didn't finish this cavern's build-out, remember? At least they piped in water for Dr. B—huge headache averted there, if the water is safe to drink. We might find the outline of other 'rooms' scribed into the walls. Private offices, perhaps, but certainly places for the President's staff and the President himself to sleep."

He moved farther into the second room, toward the back. "They didn't get the place finished before they abandoned—oh, wow. Uh, *eureka?*"

"Eureka?" Bickel crowded into the second room and peered over Rick's shoulder. Beyond the niche, where the rear and left-hand walls should have met and formed a corner, the rear wall stopped short of meeting up with the wall on their left, but the left-hand wall continued on into darkness.

Rick grinned. "I don't see a glow-in-the-dark EXIT sign, Doc, but I'm pretty sure this has to be it."

Bickel vibrated with excitement. "Come on, boys. Let's see where this goes."

Bickel stepped through and took an immediate right, shined his light into the start of yet another passageway. When he'd walked about six yards, it opened to a respectable width. As Bickel reached a hard left turn, the beam of his flashlight struck the wall facing him, and he came to a stop.

"Feast your eyes on *this*."

About eighteen inches in diameter, the seal of the President of the United States gleamed back at them.

⌘

HAVING FEWER TWISTS and turns, the route to the surface was more direct than the construction passageway had been. Conversely, the route was considerably steeper than the one they'd used to first enter the cavern. Bickel thought the passage headed due west, crossing above the cavern, going on for a distance.

To mitigate what would have been a steep slope, the builders had carved steps and landings into the inclines. Bickel practically raced up the steps on his thin legs, Rick and Tony right behind him.

He was nonplussed when he found himself staring at a solid rock wall. The tunnel had come to an abrupt and unforgiving end.

"This can't be right," he said to the air. "This cannot be right!"

"You're correct, Doc. The tunnel has to go on from here and the exit must be near, given how far we've come. May I?" Rick asked.

Tony was already pushing forward, as determined as Rick to find the answer. They started on opposite sides of the wall, shining their lights over every inch of rock, moving their fingertips across the rough stone surface.

Fifteen minutes passed before Rick exclaimed, "Think I've got something." He pointed to a slender crack near his boot tip. "Look here. See this crack? I think it's actually the space between two stones."

"Two completely smooth stones," Tony added, "chiseled and honed to join together."

"Yes, and if this wall was made, it might not be as solid as it looks."

"Hurry it up," Bickel groused.

"Yes, Doc," Rick answered with the patient familiarity of years.

The space between the rocks was wide enough for Rick to slide one finger into it. An inch in, he encountered a metal bar.

"I feel a lever!"

He pressed down on the piece of metal. *Nothing.*

Tried to lift it. *Nada.*

Side-to-side. *Nope.*

"What *are* you doing, Rick?" Dr. Bickel demanded.

"Trying to get this lever to move."

"Stand aside," Bickel commanded.

Rick and Tony, accustomed to Bickel's frequently imperious manner, did as he asked.

Bickel put his finger into the niche . . . and pushed the lever straight back. It stuck for a fraction of a second. Then it gave way. All three of them heard a *click* and the *whirr* of a mechanism within the wall.

"Merciful heavens!" Bickel exclaimed. "As you said, it *can't* be a solid stone wall; it's a door, *paneled in stone.*"

The heavy, ponderous door swung open on a great, silent pivot point.

The three men waited, silent and watchful, until Bickel plucked up his courage and stepped through.

"No," he said over his shoulder. "Don't follow me. We don't know where we are yet, and if this door should close behind us? Who knows if we'd be able to open it from this side?"

Rick shivered and took two steps back. "Yikes. Glad you said that."

"Yeah. What Rick said," Tony muttered, "although I do see light coming from somewhere."

The pivoting door had opened from the wall of a faintly illumined tunnel. Bickel wetted his finger and held it up. He felt a gentle breeze from the left—quite common to the ventilation system inside the mountain's main tunnels. He turned right, walked forward, and reached a familiar sight: a wide iron door.

"Bunker!" he laughed to himself. He returned to Rick and Tony. "We're inside a bunker, and the exterior door is down there. We've done it! We've found the presidential route to the lost devolution site. From here on, going in and coming out should take less time and effort and be safer for us."

"Need to know how to open this door from where you're standing," Rick reminded them.

"Right you are," Bickel agreed. "Tony, you remain on that side of the door in case we can't figure this out. Rick? You're with me. We'll identify which bunker we're in, then open the door from our side."

"Uh, you want me to stay behind? By myself?" Tony asked, brows lifted high.

Bickel sneered. "*Pfft!* Don't be a child. If we haven't opened the door in fifteen minutes, open it yourself from your side."

"Right, cuz I'm not afraid of being left down here. Alone. In the cold. And the dark. To die."

"Oh, brother. Give me a break." Bickel stepped back. "Oh, and Tony? Talk to us as the door closes. I want to know if we can hear you after it shuts."

"What should I say? 'Don't abandon me here alone'? How about, 'Leaving me behind is inhumane'? Say something like that?"

Bickel rolled his eyes. "Recite the periodic table or Pi to one hundred digits. Anything trivial."

Tony began with the states and their capitals in alphabetical order. He rambled on, while Bickel and Rick stood on the bunker side of the door. They pushed the cumbersome door toward Tony and watched it settled into the wall, its edges disappearing as it closed.

In the same instant, Tony's recitation went silent.

"Brilliant construction," Bickel grinned. He put his light near one of the seams. "Not a blessed thing—not a visible crack or the mark of a tool. No wonder this door has remained a secret!"

"Shall we open the bunker door? See where we are?"

"Yes. Let's."

They slowly pushed open the door. When they peered out into the dark sky, the lights of Kirtland and the Albuquerque Sunport lit up the distant sky.

"We're on the west side of the mountain!" Rick exclaimed. "We went in on the southeast side and crossed over to the west."

"Did you catch the bunker number? Yes? Let's get back inside, shall we? And I suggest that we strategically remove the closest lightbulbs to this door. That will keep it dark as we're entering and leaving."

He and Rick closed the bunker door and returned to the door leading to the presidential route. They ran their hands over where they *knew* the door was, ran them around its shape, even across the wall surrounding the door, looking for a seam—to no avail.

"Man, this is one tough nut," Rick muttered. "Good thing we know what to look for, right?"

"Yes, but it's getting late," Bickel said, his enthusiasm starting to fray around the edges, his energy to ebb. "Let's find the mechanism, shall we?" He focused his light along the floor where it met the wall. He slowly walked the beam to one side. Nothing. Then he started over, moving up a foot. He repeated the process two feet above the floor.

Finally saw something.

Eighteen inches from what they estimated was the edge of the invisible door, he spied minute fractures in the rock wall. "Rick, this has to be it, but they've outdone themselves with this concealment. Help me figure it out, please."

Rick came over. Ran his fingers over a faint outline about six inches high and an inch wide. When his fingers reached the top of the outline and he pressed, it gave way. Hinged near the top, the miniscule flap lifted up and revealed a lever behind it within a niche.

Rick put his finger on the lever and pushed it back. The door pivoted open, and Tony rushed out, breathing fast and heavy.

"Sheesh! Finally! Let me outta here."

⌘

ON THE DRIVE BACK to the lab, Bickel was quiet.

"You okay, Dr. B?" Tony asked.

"Right as can be, thank you. But as we have reached the devolution site and gotten inside, can we acknowledge that doing so was our most difficult and time-consuming task?"

He had their attention. "What I mean to say is that we don't need to increase the number or intensity of our nocturnal outings. Yes, we have big tasks ahead to prep the cavern as my temporary habitation, but we have time—a year, I estimate. Let's keep to our same pace. That way, I can dedicate my energy to training and improving the nanomites."

"Okay by me," Tony said.

Rick grunted his agreement.

⌘⌘⌘⌘

PART 2:
THE PERILOUS PART IN THE MIDDLE

CHAPTER 8

JANUARY

BICKEL DRAGGED HIMSELF into work Tuesday morning. Until last evening, he and his team hadn't been inside the mountain for three weeks. Their last scheduled foray had been postponed due to Sandia's regular closure over Christmas and New Year's.

Consequently, Bickel, Rick, and Tony remained inside the mountain Monday night until 2:00 a.m. Once home, it had taken Bickel another two hours to unwind. He'd been too keyed up to sleep and had revisited the many preparations they'd made during the past year.

He found himself second-guessing what remained undone versus how much time they had left. Moreover, he fretted over how to extricate the nanomites from his lab when that time came.

As a result, he'd eked out less than two hours of rest.

Rick's chipper voice called from his workstation, "Morning, Doc!"

"Shut up."

Rick and Tony sniggered under their breath. Bickel was unquestionably smarter than the two of them put together, but they had him on stamina. They could handle skipping hours of sleep. Bickel at twenty years their senior? Not so much.

Rick poured a cup of coffee into Bickel's usual mug and took it to him. Set it on Bickel's desk.

Bickel sighed. "Thanks, Rick. And, er, sorry about my reply."

"No worries, Doc."

⌘

"DR. BICKEL, EXPLAIN again how your 'nanobots,' as you call them, will be able to 'learn' new tasks." Dr. Prochanski sat back, a coy smirk dancing on his lips.

Bickel saw the question for what it was: It was partly Prochanski's attempt at bringing Bickel to heel, of asserting his authority over him, but the greater part was Prochanski's need for Bickel to repeat what Prochanski had been too dense to follow—even after Bickel had delivered his detailed weekly presentation—inclusive of slides and handouts.

Bickel growled low in his throat. "You *can* read, can't you, Prochanski? Or is it *I* who am at fault? I assumed you learned to read somewhere along the way to your 'doctorate.' I apologize if I presumed too much."

The room went ominously quiet as the two postdocs, the other attendees at Bickel's weekly AMEMS status briefing, pulled in on themselves. In most of Bickel's briefings, Prochanski managed to insert at least one pompous or ignorant question. Invariably, Bickel couldn't resist belittling Prochanski, yanking his chain. Baiting the bear.

He snickered inwardly. *But really, how could I resist? Prochanski makes it far too easy—the arrogant buffoon.*

Bickel's fatigue may have contributed to his impatience. Ignoring the warning buzzing in his head, he doubled down. "Dear me—is it worse than that? Do you need me to translate my briefing notes? Dumb them down for you?"

He kept his attention on Prochanski, not allowing his gaze to shift toward the sole interesting person in the room, *Gemma Keyes*, Prochanski's project manager and little protégé. Bickel knew where she was without checking. She was holed up in her *de rigueur* spot, far off to the side, where she transcribed meeting notes onto her laptop. Bickel knew, too, how careful and cautious Gemma was—careful not to draw attention to herself, cautious as a mouse in a field of foxes.

She was, in fact, in the habit of making herself as small and as forgettable as possible. Practically invisible.

She rather fascinated him, if he was being honest with himself.

What is it about her? Why does her Little Miss Wallflower routine intrigue me?

As tension in the room mounted toward another all-out shouting match between Bickel and Prochanski—a match that Bickel always won—she'd be flattening herself against the conference room wall, attempting to merge into it and disappear entirely. She was so adept at this routine that people often forgot she was in the room.

For some reason, he never did.

As his mind wandered, he was able to ignore Prochanski's arrogant bleating. Ignore his rant until the man's repeated bellows snagged his attention.

"Dr. Bickel! *Dr. Bickel!* You *will* address me as *Doctor* and with proper respect, or I will have you written up!"

"Suit yourself," Bickel scoffed. "The private sector has hounded me for years, offering to build me a lab three times the size of AMEMS and, furthermore, build it to my exact specifications. The private sector hires only the best and brightest, of course. Well. I suppose that's why they're beating a path to your door, isn't it?"

Prochanski, barely controlling his rage, ground out, "That will be all for today. Dismissed."

Ignoring Prochanski and his two wet-nosed postdocs, Bickel swept up his notes and rose from his seat. He allowed himself one quick glance at Gemma. As usual, what he saw piqued his interest further: She stared, blinking, at her laptop's screen.

A more morose expression he'd never witnessed: Guilt competing with shame.

As Bickel strode away he pondered on what he'd seen, what he'd perceived.

I wonder what weighs heavily upon on you, Miss Keyes. Yes, I do wonder.

⌘

AN HOUR LATER, he had his answer: *Demure little Gemma Keyes was spying on him.* He'd hacked her work email and found the weekly reports Prochanski demanded of her. Became aware of her amateur attempts to cozy up to him on Prochanski's behalf.

Bickel wasn't angry. Not at her at any rate. In fact, he felt a measure of sorrow for the young woman. He could envision the pressure Prochanski used to manipulate her.

You've been spying on me for that toad, have you, Gemma? Recording my comings and goings, attempting to account for every moment of my time, then reporting back to Prochanski?

I can't fault you, I suppose. Your conscience seems to be doing a fine job of that. Besides, Prochanski has you under his thumb, doesn't he? He could get rid of you in a snap if you refused to follow his orders.

But I think you hate it, Gemma, because you aren't terribly good at dissembling—not when it goes against your ingrained values.

Bickel snorted softly, coming to a decision. He opened his classified safe and withdrew a sealed envelope. Slit it open. A sheet of black dots, each the size of a pencil eraser, dropped into his hand. He peeled one from the sheet and slipped it into his pocket.

FYI, between me and thee, Gemma? Two can play at your little game.

He left his office door open and told his subconscious to listen for Gemma's comings and goings while he tussled his way through a particularly complex algorithm, one that stubbornly refused to produce the precise results he desired.

His head lifted when his subconscious told him Gemma had left her desk for the restroom. He sauntered from his office, crossed the lobby to the drinking fountain, then returned—passing by Gemma's cubicle. He leaned over the cubicle wall and placed one sticky black dot on the back edge of her laptop, close to her network port. The voice-activated "bug" he'd planted on her laptop would record every conversation Gemma took part in.

Even those private meetings where Gemma reports to Prochanski how and where I spent every minute of my day!

The bug had a short-range transmitter, too. It would allow Bickel, from the comfort of his office not far from Gemma's lobby cubicle, to download the bug's take and listen to it at his leisure.

Knowing Gemma would return shortly and wanting to put eyes on her without being overt, he wandered into the breakroom, grabbed a disposable cup, and filled it with coffee.

Ah. Here she comes.

But when he walked toward his office, Gemma wasn't at her desk.

She was in his office.

He was, to a point, amused. To a point.

High time to take you down a peg, Miss Keyes.

Her head snapped up when he stood in the doorway. He'd caught her in the act of snooping, and yet somehow she kept her cool. Managed a blank expression.

I suppose I can admire that in you.

With a wan smile, he said, "I hope you're being careful, Gemma."

Her unflappable poker face twitched. Then she was gone.

Bickel sat and considered the game being played—Prochanski coercing Gemma to spy on him. Bickel, turning the tables on Prochanski.

Where would it end?

His mouth tightened. *That's right, Prochanski, you worthless braggart. Two can play at your game.*

⌘⌘⌘⌘

Chapter 9

WHEN SANDIA HIRED Bickel and he relocated to Albuquerque, he bought a home inside the exclusive Tanoan Community. Considering his personal wealth and the other properties he owned across the US, it would not have surprised his acquaintances or colleagues to learn that he had paid for it outright.

What none of his friends knew—not even Rick and Tony—was that Bickel already owned a house in Albuquerque, a modest, somewhat dated ranch-style dwelling he had never lived in, a house he would normally consider beneath him. Bickel had purchased the house two years before he "arranged" for Sandia to headhunt him.

Why this house? As Bickel's vision for the nanomites matured toward a triumphant success, he also foresaw how corrupt actors within the government—General Cushing, in particular—would attempt to appropriate his work. He bought the house to serve two purposes, first, as a temporary hiding place, *a safe house*, should he need to prematurely flee with his project in hand, should he need to run before his preparations to vanish into the mountain were complete.

The house's present or past ownership would not lead back to Bickel. In point of fact, he had gone to great lengths to ensure that no one alive could connect him to the house.

Under a credible, albeit fictional, identity, Bickel had hired an older Albuquerque attorney and padded the man's upcoming retirement with an obscene amount of money—half then, half when his work for Bickel was complete. The attorney, acting on his client's instructions, formed a corporation, then a shell company under that corporation. Finally, the attorney purchased the house in the shell company's name.

The attorney then hired contractors to make modifications to the house. Those modifications were detailed and *unusual*. When the modifications were complete, Bickel flew into Albuquerque under a second assumed identity to view and approve the work. While alone in the house, he added his own finishing touches, changing out the house's entry locks, stocking supplies, and installing and configuring additional security enhancements—enhancements he would count on should he find himself on the run.

It was the first time Bickel had set foot in the house. It was the lone time *anyone* would enter the house until it was needed.

A year after purchasing the dwelling, the attorney, acting for the shell company, sold the property to a private party—a third faux identity provided by Bickel. The attorney then dissolved the corporation and its shell company and destroyed his records of both. He closed his law practice, collected the second half of his hefty fee, and moved to Cabo. Four years later, after a happy but brief retirement, the man passed away—and with him passed all firsthand knowledge of the house's provenance.

To its neighbors, the house stood unoccupied but well-tended. A landscape service maintained the yard and the house's exterior. Their fees, along with the property's utilities, taxes, and insurance, were paid through a dedicated bank account in the owner's name—an account with a balance capable of funding the house's upkeep for another two decades.

Using a credit card associated with yet another bank account under an alias, Bickel ordered the equipment, parts, and supplies he and his techs needed to furnish the cavern. He had them delivered to the house. A struggling single mom, happy to supplement her income, collected whatever mail and packages arrived at the house, Monday through Saturday, no later than 5:00 p.m.

That was the safe house's second purpose—to receive Bickel's untraceable orders.

Bickel spread out the orders to prevent a pileup of boxes on the front porch—which might arouse the neighbors' attention—and to ensure that his lone employee could manage each day's collection. The woman delivered the packages she collected to a storage unit in a shoddy facility—a facility without security cameras.

Rick, who had never heard of the single mom, visited the same facility every Sunday afternoon. He emptied the unit and left the woman's weekly cash payment, which she picked up on Mondays. Rick, in turn, brought the packages he'd collected to Bickel's house.

There, Monday evenings after work, the three of them would open a week's worth of orders. They repackaged and staged the items into manageable loads—because the requirements of Bickel's mountain lab, small though it would be, also meant he, Rick, and Tony had to cart its many and diverse parts and pieces *into* the mountain.

In this way, they made slow but steady progress—*until*. Until Bickel ascertained that Gemma was spying for Prochanski, which meant Prochanski was watching him.

"But forewarned is forearmed," he whispered to himself.

He kicked his team into high gear.

⌘

THE WEEKS SPED by in a blur for Bickel as he, Rick, and Tony increased their forays into the mountain to three or four times a week while juggling their workload in the AMEMS lab. Most nights they made their clandestine approach to the bunker entrance shortly after 10:00 p.m., dropped their loads, and left the mountain not long after.

The weekends, on the other hand, were whirlwinds of activity. The three men labored through both Friday and Saturday nights to complete their tasks.

In addition to constructing Bickel's lab, they had to furnish a living space for him. After gaining entrance to the cavern, they had slowly stocked Bickel's "pantry" with preserved foods and other necessities, enough to supply him for six months. They included an emergency stash of water should the cavern's water supply fail for some unforeseen reason.

They furnished his kitchen with dishes and cookware, and his "bedroom" with a mattress, bedding, linens, clothing, and personal hygiene items. Bathing and laundry, Bickel was chagrined to discover, would be at the mercy of a small wash tub and two kettles with which to heat water.

Washing clothes by hand would be a fresh experience for him!

Those simple, mundane undertakings were trivial when contrasted with building the lab to Bickel's specifications. Bickel's requirements stretched Rick and Tony's imaginations and required considerable time, labor, and creativity.

They began by assembling the lab's "bones" or layout—rows of tables to accommodate half a dozen workstations for Bickel's various tools. Rick and Tony were relieved to find a number of intact tables among the office furnishings piled up in the cavern. Neither of them had relished the prospect of manhandling tables through the passages into the mountain. When they needed additional tables, they cannibalized discarded desks and cobbled together three more.

⌘

"OKAY, I HAVE ALL the workstation space I need," Bickel said, "but I insist that we declutter the lab area. Please shift the extra desks, chairs, and miscellaneous bits of office furniture to the far end of the cavern."

"Stack them along the back wall?" Rick asked.

"I have no preference," Bickel called over his shoulder, "as long as you clear my lab area."

Rick and Tony carried the odd remnants of furniture to the cavern's back "corner," piling smaller pieces atop larger ones. They labored until they had cleared Bickel's designated lab space to his satisfaction. As they finished, Rick, hands on his hips, considered the five old file cabinets they'd lined up along the cavern's back wall.

"I could use one of those at home. Not as though I'd be stealing from the government, right? They did abandon them."

"Oh, yeah," Tony scoffed. "Why not? We'll drop one of these monsters into our commandeered Sandia van and haul it back to the AMEMS parking lot. Then you can decide how to get it into the trunk of your itty bitty Nissan."

"Oh, yeah. Guess that would be a problem. Maybe there's a short one around."

"Maybe."

Tony left to help Bickel wrestle tables into the most recent configuration he'd decided on, while Rick wandered through the piles of furniture. Not finding what he was looking for, Rick started toward Bickel's lab area. He glanced sideways toward the rugged back wall of the cavern. Stopped. Tipped his head. Squinted.

Where the rough stone "wall" touched the cavern's "floor," a length of craggy rock shelf protruded. Something to the right of that shelf had caught his eye.

He needed to get up closer to it and squat down before he realized that the protrusion was *an overhang*, and what he initially accepted as solid rock behind the protrusion was *a skinny, dark fissure* about three feet high.

"Hello. What have we here?"

He pointed his flashlight into the fissure. Its beam penetrated about six feet before the crack closed up.

Or did it?

I'd like a closer look-see.

Rick, a rather tall man, would need to get on his hands and knees to squeeze through the fissure's skinny mouth. He put the butt of his small flashlight in his mouth, the lighted end pointing forward. Seeing rock where the split ended, but curious nonetheless, he crawled in—and found that beyond the mouth, the crack widened.

When he hit the end of the fissure . . . the "crack" made an abrupt 90-degree right turn, *straight into the mountain—not* a rock's natural behavior.

"What in the world!"

He pointed his light into the turn and, to his amazement, found that what should have been solid stone opened up, both wider and higher. Once he crawled through, he was able to stand. He pointed his light down an unmistakably human-made passage.

The light glinted off something. He moved ahead to see what it was.

A door. A rough and rusted iron door. A door without a handle.

"Great. Another locked door. I'm thrilled."

He *was* intrigued, though.

He played the light over the door's surface, then down the stone on both sides. Near the bottom on the left, he spied a crack or crevice about a finger's width wide. He pushed his index finger into the crevice and immediately encountered a length of smooth metal.

"Ah-ha! Betcha I know how you work." Like the door on the presidential route, the lever moved straight back when he pushed on it.

He heard the *snick* of the mechanism, then the unmistakable sound of a lock clicking open. The door, on soundless hinges, swung away from him.

He grinned. "Excellent."

The yawning tunnel beyond him beckoned.

Rick shook his head. "Nope. Not this sucker. I am *not* gonna let this door lock behind me. No, sir!"

With one foot holding the door open, he ran the flashlight's beam down the other side's door jamb, then over the stone surface to the side of the jamb. There he saw two rocks—more like fitted bricks— and a crack between them. The rocks and crack mirrored those on the other side.

He squatted and put a finger into the crack, encountered the expected metal lever, and pushed it in. He heard the mechanism move, and the lock click. He shivered, recalling how far *down* inside the mountain the cavern was.

"This lever will likely open the door from either side. On the other hand, self-preservation is high on my list of priorities. Call me paranoid if you want, but I don't intend to get trapped down here."

He pulled his wallet from his rear pocket, let the door almost close, then stuffed his wallet between the door and jamb, effectively keeping the door ajar..

He pulled his wallet from his rear pocket, let the door almost close, then stuffed his wallet between the door and jamb, effectively keeping the door ajar.

"Makes sense to me that the designers of a presidential devolution site would provide the President with another way out—should it be needed. Well, Doc could use an emergency exit. Let's see where this goes, shall we?"

He moved on.

⌘⌘⌘⌘

CHAPTER 10

BICKEL TURNED IN A circle, scanning the cavern. "Tony, where's Rick?"

"He's . . ." Tony's head swiveled to his left, then his right. "He was with me in the back."

"You mean forty minutes ago when you finished moving the furniture?"

"Was it that long? Well, he can't be far. This place isn't *that* big."

Tony lifted his voice and called out, "Hey, Rick? Where are you, dude?"

Nothing but silence answered him.

Bickel and Tony walked the perimeter of the cavern calling for Rick, to no avail. When they had scoured every nook and cranny, including the toilet stall, they stared at each other.

"Where's Rick, Dr. B?"

"Your guess is as good as mine, Tony."

"Yeah, but what do we do about him?"

Bickel rubbed his chin and didn't answer.

⌘

SIX FEET FARTHER, the tunnel took a left and shrank down to a width Rick wasn't convinced he'd fit through. Oh, it was plenty tall but thin. He shined his light into the narrow crack and wondered if it, like the fissure, made another turn.

"Give it a go, Rick," he told himself. "But back out if it narrows even a hair more."

He turned sideways and skinned along inside the crack. After a few terrifying feet, it *did* turn. A dozen inches later, it turned again, back on itself. Like a tight "s."

Then he was through, sliding out from "behind" a wall, into another wide passageway—a passageway that, if you didn't know about the "behind the wall" part, would at first blush seem a dead end.

He shook his head. *Cool beans. Whoever designed this route disguised it coming and going.*

Facing the single way forward left open to him, he walked on. The passage continued on for quite a while, sloping ever upward.

Rick was relieved. *Up is good.*

Eventually, though, he reached another "end," a jagged opening two and a half feet high, a foot wide, and about a foot off the stone floor, a crevice he was not convinced he could—or would *want* to—try squeezing himself through.

The funny thing, though? He was sure he saw a faint glow coming through the small fissure.

He switched off his flashlight. Right. A dim light came from the crack. He squatted and peered through. Something—a support beam?—stood directly in front of the crevice, blocking his view. He caught a glimpse to his left.

What he saw? Blew him away.

A tunnel, big and high enough to drive a semi through. A tunnel with huge struts and support beams on either side. A tunnel he was certain he'd never ventured into, but a tunnel, nonetheless.

If I manage to squeeze through, then I'm out in the open? Nope. Not gonna do that.

He pulled back, debating whether he should return to the cavern.

But why would this route end here? What if, instead of ending, the route continues on the other side of this tunnel? What if there's another crack, behind another beam, and the President's secret escape route goes on from there?

He pushed himself through the crack, left leg first, shoulder and arm following. He grabbed the edge of the beam and dragged the rest of himself through, scraping off some skin in the process.

Strings of electric lights mounted along the walls lit the tunnel— just as they did in every other part of the facility. He lifted his head and listened. Nothing. Not a whisper, not a hum. He bent down and, with the end of his flashlight, scribed a small, horizontal mark on the beam near the floor.

"Not getting lost underground," he told himself for the umpteenth time.

Then he wasted no time. He scooted to the other side of the tunnel, checked behind the beam. No crack. Moved on to the next one. No crack.

Two beams later, he found what he was looking for. After making a similar mark on the beam, he pushed himself through the crack and moved on.

The rest of his journey took minutes. It ended at yet another old iron door. This door had a visible locking mechanism that spanned the back of the door, a wheel connected to a series of flat bars. He spun the wheel and turned it in a half circle. The bars moved, and bolts, top and bottom, retracted into the door's thick core.

The door opened out, and a breeze struck him. Through the open doorway, Rick saw a cluster of tall rock pillars.

"Hey, I'm outside! Somewhere on the mountain, but outside!"

He stepped over the threshold onto sand. The rocks around him formed a natural pocket that hid the door. He took a step toward the lowest of the rocks, hoping to look over it and pinpoint his location.

The *snick* of the door closing behind him announced his mistake. He ran back to it, but it had no handle to grab. To add insult to injury, he heard the bolts sliding home, locking him out.

"You stupid *bleeping* rookie!"

⌘

WHEN RICK POPPED out from the direction of what would be Bickel's bedroom, Bickel and Tony were seated at Bickel's little dinette table, their abject expressions almost comical.

"Hey, guys. Miss me?"

Tony gaped. Then he jumped up. "I'm gonna kill you! Where have you been? And how . . . how did you get past us?"

"First? I'm parched." Rick went to the kitchen sink and poured himself a glass, guzzled it. Chugged a second.

Bickel hadn't moved, but he eyed Rick with tamped-down anger. "Sit down."

Rick sat.

"Where'd you get off to, Rick?"

"I found another way out, Doc, probably a last-ditch escape route for the President. I followed it to where it opened, behind a bunch of big rocks on the northeast side of the mountain, a couple hundred feet up the slope from the road that connects the bunkers."

"And?"

Rick sighed. "Let the door close behind me. Couldn't get back inside. So, I did what I had to do. Hiked down to the road, jogged about four miles back around to our car, then came back inside. By the way? I'm starving."

Bickel's eyes gleamed. "Another route, eh? Comes out on the northeast side of the mountain, you say?"

"A quarter of a mile from the northern point of the mountain on the east side."

"I'm going to need you to document that route, Rick."

"Sure thing, Doc, but perhaps we need to think bigger."

"Bigger?"

"Yes. Include a direct route all the way *off the base*. From that door, down the slope, through the PIDAS, then over to the base fence and out."

"Good idea. I leave it to you to figure out how to get through the PIDAS and the base perimeter fence and document it all—but get it done quickly, can you? Leave the details in my desk over there."

"I can do that. Uh, need to retrieve my wallet first." His smile was sheepish. "Used it as a door stop on the first door I encountered—then let the second door get the best of me."

"Your best must not be all that good," Tony growled. "By the way? You about gave me a heart attack."

"Sorry, man."

The two friends hugged, and Bickel stood.

"Get your wallet, Rick, then let's get out of here. We've had enough fun for one day."

⌘⌘⌘⌘

Chapter 11

WHEN BICKEL MADE his jump to his "laboratory under the mountain," the nature of his work would no longer be R&D. Rather, he would prepare the nanomites to greet the world.

Bickel intended to build a computer interface between himself and the nanomites and establish meaningful communication with them.

To that end, Bickel and his men had, over the past months, upgraded the cavern's electrical panel and installed a server, a series of computers networked via the server, two scanners, and a laser printer. They also hauled in, set up, and calibrated two costly microscopes—a scanning electron microscope and a high-powered 3D laser microscope, each with its own dedicated workstation.

The focal point of the lab, however, was a transparent cube, its sides and top composed of commercial-grade tempered glass. It wasn't an ordinary glass case, by any stretch of the imagination. Bickel and his techs had assembled the glass panels and sealed their joints, then used specially made HEPA filters to remove particulates until the glass interior was as pristine as a submicron cleanroom. The case itself sat on a sturdy base that lifted the case off the stone floor . . . where it waited for its occupants to arrive.

While Prochanski drove Bickel and his team to hit their AMEMS goals, he had no idea how far ahead they actually were. Nor did he "get" the purpose of Bickel's 3D printer, a printer equipped with an innovation of Bickel's own design—a nanopore print head—possibly the greatest breakthrough of Bickel's career. The print head enabled Bickel's 3D printer to extrude liquid polymers and metals one atom at a time onto a thin wafer of silicon substrate.

Bickel had intentionally withheld knowledge of the print head from Prochanski.

Fortunately, as long as Bickel continued to report ample progress, Prochanski was happy to leave him to his work. Prochanski himself, on the other hand, seemed distracted, preoccupied, and Bickel could not escape his growing sense of unease.

"What's up with that guy?" Rick asked Bickel, jutting his chin in Prochanski's direction.

"I haven't figured that out yet, Rick, but whatever it is? It won't be good. We must proceed as though it is nefarious. We cannot assume otherwise."

He waved Tony over. "Keep our printer going as many hours each day as possible without overworking it."

Tony nodded. "We'll keep it spitting out more of our tiny tribe members while Prochanski is looking the other way."

Rick sniffed. "Right. Can't let Prochanski know about the little guys."

"Thank you both, but let's not personify the nanomites, all right? We shouldn't forget that they are submicron machines—yes, machines uniquely equipped to acquire information and learn from it—but machines nonetheless."

"Sure, Dr. B," Tony replied.

"In the meantime, I must complete my means of transferring them from here to the mountain without damaging them. You two keep running the printer."

"You got it, Doc," Rick said.

⌘

BICKEL'S SENSE OF foreboding intensified. To quell his mounting concerns, he pushed his techs hard and himself harder. The long hours wore on the three men both physically and mentally, and it made for short tempers—usually Bickel's.

Then, unexpectedly, Tony balked.

"Sorry, Doc. I can't work tonight. Moreover, I'm going home at five o'clock, straight up. Promised my wife I'd be on time for dinner."

"What? You can't work tonight? But you must!"

"Look, Dr. B, I gotta tell you, my wife has had it up to here with my staying out half the night a couple of times a week and most of the weekend, and me falling asleep right after dinner when I *am* home. She and I haven't had a date and I haven't spent time with my kids in months. Something's got to give, and I don't want it to be my marriage."

Bickel frowned, his temper rising. "Is that so?"

Tony shrugged. "Yeah, it is."

Bickel queried Rick. "And you?"

"Me? Oh, I'm fine . . . except the kids are starting to ask me who I am when I come through the door—that is, if they're not already in bed when I get home."

Bickel blinked slowly. "I had no idea."

Tony spread his hands. "You're not married, Doc. Not a parent. Look, we're with you all the way, but we're wearing thin. And our families didn't buy into this. What makes it worse is that they don't understand, and we can't explain."

"Ditto," Rick murmured.

Bickel said nothing. He nodded and turned inward. When Rick and Tony realized they'd lost his attention, they shrugged and returned to their tasks.

⌘

THE NEXT DAY, before the workday ended, Bickel called Rick and Tony into his office and closed the door behind them before he took his seat behind his desk. "Listen, um, I've been thinking about our schedule and how I've been driving us. Er, driving you."

The two men nodded and waited.

"We don't know how much longer I have here," Bickel said, "and I don't underestimate the ongoing risks you take for the sake of my work. Regardless, I want to do right by you both. You know I've seeded an IRA for each of you and established college funds for your children, but those are for the future."

He slid two envelopes across his desk. "Please accept these small tokens of my esteem. I acknowledge that they are mere gestures, given how you have stuck by me through the years, but I'd like your families to know that I appreciate them and their sacrifices as well as yours. I planned it out yesterday—something tangible for all of you in the *near* future."

He nudged the envelopes closer to them. "Go on. Open them."

Rick and Tony withdrew similar full-color brochures and single sheets of paper, computer printouts, and unfolded them. Rick was struck dumb; Tony found his voice first.

"Is this for real?"

"It's real," Bickel replied, and for some reason his eyes stung a little. "I estimate we will finish all of our preparations no later than mid-May, certainly before June rolls around. In a pinch, we can be done by April, but May would be preferable. Any time after that . . . if you can hang with me until then?"

"But . . . *an African Safari?* For—" Rick fought the clog stuck in his throat. "For my entire family?"

"Yes, and it's far less than you deserve! The two of you and your families can go together or go separately, whichever you prefer. Call that number to book your safari dates."

Tony folded the paper and put it and the brochure back in the envelope. Licked his lips. "Thank you, Dr. Bickel. Driving alongside lions, giraffes, zebras, and rhinos? It's the trip of a lifetime! My kids are gonna flip, and I . . ." He shook his head. "Thank you, Dr. B."

Rick sniffed. "Ditto, Doc."

⌘

WITH RENEWED DETERMINATION, Bickel and his men pressed ahead, checking off each task or item as the days flew by. What was missing was a reliable, high-speed internet connection.

Bickel had already subscribed to a satellite internet service provider. What the ISP required was a signal receiver somewhere atop the mountain and a means of feeding that signal into the cavern. Since no satellite signal could penetrate the mountain, they had spent many hours brainstorming how they might bring the signal into the cavern.

Bickel had acquired a set of the ventilation schematics years ago from the daughter of a deceased contractor foreman. The man had been the engineer in charge of the mountain facility's ventilation system. The schematics did not indicate where the ductwork branched off and fed the cavern—but by triangulating the cavern's vents to the ductwork above, they were able to guestimate, then locate, where the cavern's ductwork intersected the main ventilation system.

It was Tony who made the confident announcement. "We can do this, Dr. B. See this tunnel junction here, and the chimney that runs up and out of the mountain?"

Bickel checked the diagram. The "chimney" Tony indicated was massive, a ten-foot-square concrete structure that rose from the tunnel floor and exited a shoulder of the mountain into open air. A giant, engine-driven fan at the base of the chimney sucked air in from the outside and fed it into a series of ducts.

"The entire facility draws fresh air directly from that chimney—as does your cavern. We need to run coax cable from your cavern all the way up that chimney, into open air outside the mountain, and mount your ISP's satellite receiver to the outside of the chimney."

Bickel stroked his scraggly chin hairs. "The designers of this devolution site would have considered that chimney an unacceptable risk to the President, wouldn't they? If enemy planes bombed the mountain, wouldn't that have severed the President's source of air—or allowed radioactive contamination to flow into the command center? That's not the standard of engineering I would have expected for a presidential devolution site."

"Right, but that's why they built a cutoff point here." Tony tapped the schematic to point it out. "Literally, they could seal off that ventilation shaft with the press of a button."

"And that button is where?"

"Haven't found it yet, but, *hey*—we're not expecting a bomber to drop its payload over the mountain, are we?"

"How was the President supposed to breathe if they sealed off the air shaft?"

"Oh, that's easy. See the ductwork here where it branches off about twenty feet up from the cavern? That branch leads to a secondary intake point. You've got two sources of fresh air coming into the cavern at all times."

"They did think of everything," Bickel admitted.

"Yup. Redundancies built into all their planning. Too bad thermonuclear bombs came into vogue after they built this facility. One of those would have killed the entire mountain. Otherwise, the government might not have abandoned these devolution sites.

"Anyway, I estimate I could carry a roll of coax cable to the top of the shaft, then unwind and attach the cable to the chimney's wall as I come down. From the trailing end of the cable at the base of the chimney, Rick or I would attach another length of cable and feed it down the ventilation shaft to the cavern."

Bickel snorted. "And will you walk on water while you're at it? The schematics say that chimney is more than a hundred feet straight up!"

"One hundred fifteen feet, to be exact." Tony pointed to the schematic. "See this ladder attached to a wall inside the chimney? One hundred fifteen feet on a ladder is definitely a climb and a half. I'll wear a safety harness and attach myself to the ladder as I move up. And actually? Running cable up and out isn't the tricky part."

His finger pointed to a spot on the schematic. "The tricky part comes after we drop the cable into the ductwork leading to the cavern.

Right here, the ductwork takes a 90-degree turn. We can't push cable past that point. We'll need to send someone into the ductwork from the cavern, navigate to that point right there, snag the cable, and pull it the rest of the way into the cavern."

"You can do that?" Bickel asked. "Crawl all that way inside the ductwork?"

Tony laughed. "Nope. The ductwork is too small for either Rick or me, but Sparks can do it."

Bickel blinked in confusion. "Sparks? How could *sparks* grab and pull a cable?"

Rick and Tony chuckled. They chortled and guffawed until tears streaked their faces. And when they saw Bickel's ire building, they pointed and laughed harder.

Tony got it together enough to say, "Sorry, Doc. See, Sparks is my wee Scottish Terrier."

"Terrier? You're sending *a dog* into the ventilation system? To retrieve a *cable?*"

"Yup. I'll attach a lightweight leader line to the end of the cable and tie the line to his favorite pull toy. Sparks and I play fetch with that toy. I'll practice running him through a length of pipe to retrieve his toy, then fasten the toy to a line and practice having him bring me his toy *and* the extra weight of the line. See, when he brings us that line, we can pull it and the cable into the cavern ourselves."

"That far into the ducts, how will, er, *Sparks* even see his toy?"

"We'll drop a glow stick down the shaft to guide him in. Don't worry—he'll do it."

⌘

THE FOLLOWING WEEKEND, while Rick kept watch, Tony climbed the chimney, carrying tools and a heavy-duty, solar-powered satellite receiver in a pack on his back. At the top, he encountered an iron grate, chained and locked, guarding the chimney's mouth. The chain and lock were rusted from the elements.

With his harness and backpack clipped to the ladder, Tony used his battery-powered grinder to cut through one link of the chain. He removed the link, pulled the chain out of the grate, and secured the link and the chain in a pouch around his waist. Then he heaved the hinged grate open and climbed out of the chimney—far enough to bend over its side.

His next task was to bolt the satellite receiver and its solar panel to the exterior wall of the chimney. Both the receiver and solar panel were small, less than a foot each, and he and Rick had painted them a mottled buff color that would blend in to the mountain terrain.

He finished his tasks, powered the receiver on, set it to receive the pre-coded signal, and tested the signal's strength. When he climbed back down, his legs and feet were quivering from fatigue.

"Gotta take a break, Rick."

"Let's go back to the cavern. Get you lunch."

"And three or four ibuprofen."

⌘

AN HOUR LATER, they returned to the chimney. Tony stretched his aching legs and feet, while Rick eyed him with concern.

"Sure you can do this in one go, dude?" Rick asked.

"What I'm sure of is that my feet will tell me later how badly I mistreated them," Tony groaned, "but I can do it. I'll soak them in ice water tonight."

He repeated his climb to the top of the chimney, this time with the leading end of a long coil of cable attached to his toolbelt—the cable's length hanging down to the bottom of the chimney—and a six-foot piece of cable in his pouch. First he connected one end of the short cable to the receiver. Then he pulled the grate closed and pulled the short cable through. He threaded the chain through the grate. He brought the two ends together, added the broken link, and "fused" the link with epoxy. A discerning eye *might* notice the seam in the link.

He then connected the end of the long cable snaking down the chimney to the short cable attached to the receiver and bolted the joined pieces to the concrete chimney. After an hour-and-a-half of bolting the length of the cable down the wall, from top to bottom, his legs and feet were cramping painfully. He climbed down the final rungs and collapsed on the stone floor.

"Ow."

Rick shook his head. "Ya think?"

⌘

TONY BROUGHT SPARKS to the mountain the following Friday night. The black-eyed terrier scampered about the cavern, sniffing and whiffling, but finding nothing much to interest him.

"Okay, what I'm going to do," Tony said, "is play fetch with Sparks here in the cavern, get his attention fixed on his pull toy."

Tony attached the pull toy to a length of leader line and dragged it across the floor. Sparks ran yipping after him. When Tony dropped the line and ran back to Bickel and Rick, Sparks grabbed the toy and brought it and the line to him. They practiced several times without a problem.

"Okay, let's have him retrieve his toy from the ductwork."

Tony climbed the ladder and opened the vent. Rick climbed up with Sparks peeking out of his jacket. Tony offered Sparks a bit of kibble.

"Want this, boy? See where I'm putting it?" Tony placed the treat inside the vent where Sparks could see it. Then he took Sparks in his arms. "Get it, boy."

Sparks leapt from Tony's arms into the vent and gobbled up the kibble. When Sparks finished his treat, Tony tossed the pull toy and leader line into the vent. Sparks brought the toy back, trailing the line, and Tony gave him more kibble as a reward. Tony tossed the pull toy farther with each iteration, but Sparks never failed to bring it back.

"I think we're ready. Rick, you and Dr. B will take this spool of cable to the shaft at the base of the chimney. Attach the leader line and Sparks' toy to it, and drop them, toy first, into the shaft."

"Got it," Rick replied. "I figure it will take us better than half an hour to get there."

"Let's both of us set a fifty-minute timer on our phones the moment you and Dr. B head out. When you reach the base of the chimney, connect the end of your coax cable to the cable coming down the chimney. At forty-six minutes on your timer, drop the glow stick down the ventilation shaft. At forty-seven minutes, let down the toy, leader line, and cable. Drop a bit of kibble, too. Don't worry—that stuff stinks to high heavens, and Sparks will hunt it down.

"I'll send Sparks into the ductwork at forty-nine minutes. He'll seek out the kibble, after which he'll grab his toy and come back to me."

⌘

WHEN TONY HEARD Bickel and Rick returning from their errand, he whooped a greeting.

"Dr. B? Rick? We're online!"

Dr. Bickel's lab and living quarters in the cavern were nearly ready for occupancy. In a pinch, they would serve. All that remained was for Bickel to finalize his method for removing the nanomites from the lab.

That and his escape plan.

⌘⌘⌘⌘

CHAPTER 12

MARCH 4

THE CONFERENCE ROOM was empty when Bickel strode into it and took his usual seat. No, that wasn't true. Gemma had tucked herself into the corner, about as "out of sight, out of mind" as could be managed.

Or more so than usual?

That was his first inkling that something was off. Gemma produced the meeting agendas. If *she* was in the least way apprehensive, something had to be going down.

He wiped a hand across his tired face. Too many late nights, not enough sleep. Not even time to shower and put on clean clothes every day. The preceding night, he, Rick, and Tony had returned to the lab parking lot around 3:00 a.m.

He'd taken to bringing extra clothing to work, catching a few of hours sleep on the sofa in the breakroom, then changing into one of the suits hanging in his office—being careful not to put on the clothes he'd worn the day before. The trouble was, he'd worn the three sets of clothes about three times each. Rumpled was his novel look.

We'd better skip a couple nights in the cavern and catch up on sleep and laundry before someone notices. Then he laughed to himself. *If anyone has noticed, it'll be Gemma.*

He slid his gaze over to where she sat—frozen, as motionless as a prey animal when it sensed danger.

"Where is everyone, Gemma?"

Her answer came back, low and shaky. "I'm certain the, um, other attendees will be along shortly, Dr. Bickel."

She was nervous, all right.

Bickel checked the conference room clock. It read 10:00 a.m. straight up, and no one else had joined them yet. He turned his gaze back to Gemma, but she had her chin tucked in and her head bent over her laptop.

He sighed. *That works for ostriches, not people, Gemma—and then only in myths.*

The door to the conference room flew open as Dr. Prochanski made his typical bombastic entrance. The volume of his greeting was about as subtle as a sonic boom.

"Sorry to keep you waiting, Doctor!"

Bickel said nothing as another individual followed Prochanski into the conference room. She was as short as he remembered her, although her waistline had thickened and her once-dark hair was a striking silver, braided and knotted at the nape of her neck.

"Hello, Danny. How lovely to see you again."

Bickel flinched inside, his reaction deep and visceral. Even after more than three decades, that voice grated on his heart like fingernails on a chalkboard. Nonetheless, his stony expression did not alter. The iron grip he exerted over his expression kept his reaction hidden.

"*Imogene.* I wasn't expecting to see you today."

Or ever, if I had any say in the matter.

A host of memories flooded his mind, as well as the painful feelings he thought he'd banished forever. He shuddered under their onslaught.

⌘

Virginia Tech
Thirty-Five Years Earlier

"Students, you will need partners for this lab. Please take five minutes to pair up—with the understanding that whomever you choose will be your lab partner for the entire semester unless one of you drops the course."

Bickel sighed. The course was Physical Inorganic Chemistry and its accompanying lab. The instructor's announcement was the same song and dance.

Pick a partner you'll be saddled with for the entire semester, he sniffed. *I have carried every lab partner I've had so far through my undergrad program, but do I get credit for that?*

He snorted in derision. *I need a lab partner like I need a migraine. Maybe I'll get lucky and the lab will have an odd number of enrolled students.*

No such luck.

"Hello. I think we took the lab for polymer science together spring semester. Want to pair up?"

Bickel frowned and turned toward the voice. The comely young woman standing before him was petite with curling dark hair and bright, dancing eyes.

His mouth sort of dropped open.

She smiled, and dimples popped out near the corners of her mouth. "I'm Imogene. You're Daniel Bickel, right?"

Bickel had trouble unsticking his tongue from the roof of his mouth. "Yes. Yes, I am."

"Well? What do you say? Partners?"

Bickel managed, "Uh . . . I guess so."

The dimples ebbed and her formerly dancing eyes flashed. "Don't get overly enthusiastic on my account."

"No! I mean, *yes*. Lab partners. Sure."

Her gaze narrowed. "You'd better pull your own weight. I won't stand for procrastination or you leaving me to pick up your slack."

Bickel snapped out of his fog. "What?"

"You heard me."

"Let me set your mind at ease, *Imogene*. I'm at the top of this class and every other class I take—all twenty-one credits last semester and twenty-two this semester. I CLEPed out of every introductory math, physics, and science class the university offers. I wouldn't be taking *this* class if I had a means of testing out of it. The sooner I get all this undergrad nonsense out of the way, the sooner I can start my doctoral research."

Her dark eyes drilled deep into his, and Bickel experienced a disconcerting sensation, like he was being probed. After a moment, though, the dimples again revealed themselves—and a tidy row of very white and oddly sharp little teeth emerged with them.

He couldn't look away. *But Grandma, what sharp teeth you have!*

He chuckled nervously. "Shall we get started?"

"Yes."

They worked harmoniously while saying little—which was his preference—until they had completed the assigned tasks.

Nevertheless, he was intrigued and, after the lab ended, he accepted her invitation to grab a coffee. It was over that supposedly insignificant ritual that he was shocked to realize she was flirting. And that wasn't the most shocking part. No, the shocking part was when he found himself flirting back.

He thought she was making conversation when she asked him about his degree program and life goals. Much later, he would look back and note the signs—how she angled for him like a pro, dangling the right bait, the perfect come-hither cues.

"My goals?" Bickel had no misgivings on that score. "In fifteen or twenty years, I'll be the world's foremost expert on nanotechnology."

What set the hook was her response. "Nanotechnology? I like the sound of that. Is it a new field? Explain, please."

He was amazed at how he was dying to impress her. "*Nano*, from the nanoscale, measurements of one to one hundred nanometers. In layman's terms, very small things. Submicron. Unseen by the human eye or even a common microscope. Nanotechnology will cross the boundaries of all fields of science—physics, chemistry, biology, material science, engineering, even medicine—and incorporate them all."

Her pupils dilated. "My field is engineering. Tell me more, please. For example, how will this nanotechnology impact engineering?"

"We are basically," he said slowly, "talking about manipulation at the molecular level—manufacturing at that level."

"But no one can *see* anything that small!" She might have been challenging him, but Bickel could tell she wanted him to demolish her objections.

So he did. "Binnig and Rohrer recently announced their development of a new tool, the scanning tunneling microscope. It will allow us to see at the submicron level. They will probably win the Nobel Prize in physics for their design!

"Of course, that's only the beginning. Two to four decades should bring us fully into the realm of nanotechnology where we can manufacture machines and devices at the molecular level, even combining those devices with the human body."

She leaned closer, her breath as sweet as her smile. "To what end?"

"Why, to-to-to *fix* things, of course. To remove toxins from the bloodstream? Excise cancers? Repair congenital defects or repair other injuries?"

He heard her breath catch in her throat. "You'll put tiny 'nano things' in the body and tell them what to do?"

"Certainly."

"And you intend to be the world's foremost authority in this field? You have the intellect and drive to do this?"

Bickel was certain of two things: First, he was nearly always the smartest person in the room. Second? His drive to succeed was far greater than anyone he'd encountered to date.

*That's what I thought back then. Before I knew **her** ambition had mine beat—hands down.*

"Oh, I'll do it, all right. By the time I master physics, chemistry, and material science, I'll have clear direction on how to meld those disciplines at the nanometer level. I'll be the first to manufacture true nano devices, microscopic machines that can work for the good of humanity."

He found himself abashed by his uncharacteristic disclosures. Never had he been so open with another person, and he badly wanted to change the subject.

"Uh, what about you? It seems we might, um, share a passion for science?"

"Of course, I love everything about science. However, my dual undergrad degrees are in liberal arts and engineering," she smiled. "So you see, science is somewhat ancillary to my interests . . . Danny."

It was the first time she'd called him Danny, and he lost his heart to her in that moment. Despite her odd teeth, he hung on every smile she bestowed on him, every impish gleam of her eye. On the other hand, he couldn't grasp how anyone with such obvious talent would speak of science as 'ancillary' to anything.

"Pardon me for asking, but doesn't a liberal arts degree pair oddly with engineering?"

"Oh, the liberal arts degree is a requirement, I'm afraid. I'm an AFROTC cadet. Reserve Officers' Training Corp, Air Force. The program pays for a liberal arts degree, but I qualified for a waiver and they are paying for both. I'll be commissioned as an officer when I graduate."

You could have hit him with a brick and he wouldn't have noticed. "You're military? You choose a military career over science?"

Her reply was mild. "Why not? Doesn't the military need good engineers and scientists or, at the least, officers who know and understand science and technology, who can put it to good use?"

"Depends on what you mean by 'good use,'" he mumbled.

She laughed gently, and he instantly loved the sound. "Oh, dear. The armed services are staffed by honorable and patriotic people. The military isn't the boogeyman, you know, Danny."

⌘

PROCHANSKI COUGHED INTO his hand. "I trust you are already acquainted with General Cushing, Dr. Bickel?"

Bickel's reply was icy with disdain. "I was acquainted with an Imogene Cushing once upon a time. And as in most fairy tales? Young witches who present themselves as beautiful and virtuous maidens in their youth can never keep up the disguise. They 'generally' look the part by the time they reach their crone years. Don't you agree, 'General'?"

Bickel felt a degree of satisfaction when the color drained from Cushing's face. Prochanski, in contrast, flushed scarlet at Bickel's insults. Bickel scarcely heard Prochanski's objections.

The military isn't the boogeyman, you know, Danny.

He came back to his surroundings with that phrase ringing in his ears—along with a shrill and incessant alarm in his head. He stared at the woman who had been his lover. Who had stolen the paper he'd written outlining his vision of the future, *stolen it to advance her own career.* Her duplicitous nature had revealed itself when she betrayed his confidence . . . and irreversibly scarred his heart.

Cushing kept her back ramrod straight and met his gaze. A multitude of messages passed between them before Prochanski interrupted.

"Right, then. Now that we've exchanged pleasantries, let's call this meeting to order, shall we?"

Bickel said nothing as Prochanski's fingers fluttered with the papers in front of him. After a moment, Prochanski opened a manila folder, extracted a document, and passed it across the table to Bickel.

Dr. Prochanski's big voice echoed in the nearly empty room. "Dr. Bickel, your *involvement* in the research and development work of the AMEMS lab has been outstanding. I appreciate your *contribution* to our breakthrough, the successful development of the world's first-ever *smart*, multifunctional nanobots."

Out of the corner of his eye, Bickel saw Gemma's head snap up. Prochanski and Cushing didn't notice her reaction—they didn't seem to realize that Gemma was behind them, off to the side in the corner, dutifully taking notes.

Had they not noticed she was in the room when they came in?

Had they been too focused on him, instead?

With his peripheral vision, Bickel watched disillusionment replace Gemma's usually vacant expression. Even from across the room, he felt her loyalty to Prochanski quiver, shudder, and crumble. It was painful to behold.

He looked down at his entwined fingers. *I'm sorry you had to find out about your 'hero' this way, Gemma, but better you know the truth— as distressing as it may be.*

Dr. P continued, "Under my leadership, the work of the AMEMS lab has flourished. Our results have attracted the admiration and attention of many in the federal government. Of course, I am humbled but gratified that our government has taken notice of my lab."

"*Your* leadership? *Your* lab? AMEMS wouldn't exist without me, nor would that lab. *I* designed it. You're ignorant of the names of most of the equipment in *my* lab, not to mention their uses."

Prochanski waved away Bickel's outburst. "It is time to take the obvious next step and apply *our* work to an arena where it is much needed."

"There is no 'our' work, Prochanski, you great fraud—you pretentious, ignorant *windbag*."

Cushing, too, ignored Bickel's words. "Oh dear, yes," she added, breathless and eager. "The Pentagon will fully fund the subsequent leg of AMEMS development. They are *quite* enthusiastic. We will augment Dr. Prochanski's staff with our best and brightest minds and accelerate the rate of nanobot production."

"Not with me, you won't."

Bickel pushed away from the table, stood, and sent his chair crashing into the wall. "I won't participate. *I refuse* to participate. My contract with Sandia stipulates that *none* of my research is to be transferred to the military. You already know, *dear Imogene*, that you are the last person on earth I would allow near my work nor would I allow anyone to appropriate it for military or 'national security' purposes. The matter is closed."

Bickel stormed from the conference room. It was juvenile of him; nevertheless, he experienced a thrill of pleasure from slamming the door behind him.

He was halfway down the hall when his objective reasoning caught up with him.

This is it—zero hour. The best we can do is delay a little longer, so I can implement my exit strategy. Delay long enough to get the nanomites safely out of my lab and into the refuge of the mountain.

⌘⌘⌘⌘

CHAPTER 13

BICKEL RETURNED TO his office and fired off a succinct text to Rick and Tony.

> Cushing here to take
>
> control of nanomites
>
> for military intelligence
>
> PUSHING UP DEADLINE
>
> Meet my house 7pm
>
> Delete text

He waited to see that they'd read their texts, then deleted it from his end. He also logged onto his computer, opened a window, hacked into his cell provider's database, and deleted the text on their servers.

When I met Imogene, computers were primitive. Not anything like we have today. I had no idea then that the same brilliance that enables me to write complex mathematical algorithms would lend itself to another sort of genius: computer code.

He stopped. Looked inside himself. Didn't like what he saw.

I know, I know. I'd have nothing if you hadn't gifted me with these innate abilities. I . . . I apologize. Everything I have, everything I've achieved originated in you. Not . . . me.

These short, one-way, apologetic statements were the closest thing to prayer Bickel had offered in years. He knew they weren't enough, that his heart wasn't in a "right" state with God. Bickel knew that if he pressed in any deeper, God might have choice words with him concerning his work's too-near-to-being-an-idol status.

Bickel was afraid to go there.

Probably because it's true, his conscience chimed in.

"I didn't ask you," he growled.

He turned instead to the problematic and snarled timeframe he would have to navigate—how to string Prochanski and Cushing along until he could extricate himself and the nanomites from their clutches.

His head came up at the sound of voices in the lobby—Prochanski and Cushing. The meeting had ended. He heard the light *clunk* of Gemma's laptop as she placed it on her desk.

He was curious to know what Prochanski and Cushing had discussed after he'd left the conference room though, so he connected to the little black dot on the outside of Gemma's laptop and downloaded the audio it had recorded.

When the download finished, he fast-forwarded about two thirds through the file, plugged in a pair of earbuds, and checked where the audio had landed. Fast forwarded a bit more.

There. That's the door slamming on my way out. Nice.

Cushing spoke first. "That went as you predicted, Doctor."

"Yes. Dr. Bickel is nothing if not predictable."

The squeak of wheels as a chair rolled a few inches.

"And how will you manage without Dr. Bickel's cooperation?" Cushing's voice was harder to hear. Softer.

She rolled her chair closer to Prochanski, Bickel realized. He slid the volume up a hair.

Dr. P chuckled. His voice assumed an intimate tone. "During the entirety of Dr. Bickel's tenure here at Sandia, he has kept two sets of data—one set he 'allowed' me to access and one he thinks he has hidden from me."

Bickel nodded his satisfaction. *You only think I've kept two sets of data—make that* **three** *sets, you donkey's hind end! Oh, and congrats on finding the second fake data set. I wasn't entirely certain you had the smarts to even look for it.*

Prochanski's voice dropped lower; he positively crooned, "He believes he has kept his progress secret, but he has not."

Bickel snorted a laugh. *Careful, my obtuse friend. That spider with whom you are so enamored has sucked dry better men than you!*

He snickered as he kept listening.

"The bots he has developed are adaptive, cutting edge, as you wished, and I have taken pains to copy all of his data—*his hidden data.* He doesn't know it, but his every movement in the lab has been recorded. Since he refuses to cooperate with us, I will simply assign him to other projects, and we will carry on his work without him."

Bickel heard an insistent tapping on the conference room table—Cushing's fingernail?

"Doctor, oh, my *dear* Petrel, I must confess that I have quite the unsettled feeling about all this. The nanobots are too precious, too important to trust to Dr. Bickel in his present state of mind—don't you agree? I sense that we need to protect them, perhaps remove them from Dr. Bickel's oversight sooner than we planned. What do you think?"

A chill washed over Bickel. It raced down his back when he heard Prochanski's reply.

"If that's what you think is best, Imogene, then yes. Of course, Dr. Bickel might present a problem for us when we remove the nanobots from him. He has many powerful friends in the scientific community, you know, and he would likely raise an outcry. I take it you've managed the contractual issues he spoke of so that the legal end is covered?"

Instead of answering, Cushing sighed and murmured, "Still, we might consider whether if, at this time, Dr. Bickel has served his purpose altogether."

The chill running down Bickel's back froze solid. Even his breath staggered to a halt.

"Yes, yes! I confess that I have similar concerns. I'm confident that, with the proper resources, I can oversee the development of the nanobots to the desired level—but what if he destroys them out of spite before we can rescue them from his hands? He has, I believe, the will to act precipitately. Thus, I do agree, as we've discussed previously, that we should consider how to, ah, *remove* Dr. Bickel . . . permanently."

Bickel's thumb dropped onto the spacebar of its own accord, pausing the playback, his gaze fixed on the back wall of his office. Slowly, enunciating each word, he said, "Merciful heavens. They intend to kill me."

He sucked in a ragged breath. Shook his head to clear the shock. "No. Nope. They aren't smart enough to beat me." Then he growled in his throat. "I'll turn the tables of their own cursed game on them and—"

He shuddered with sudden trepidation. But not for himself.

"Oh, Gemma!"

He saw the young woman in his mind's eye, pressed into the corner, head down, quiet as a mouse. Overlooked and essentially invisible. His attention jumped to the audio file on his laptop. To the marker indicating the minutes remaining.

*Prochanski and Cushing don't realize Gemma is in the room— behind them, off to the side, taking notes, attentive to every word of their despicable plan! And if they are willing to off **me**, they won't bat an eye at taking **her** out! I have to do something; I have to—*

"I have to finish listening to this file."

His thumb touched the space bar and the recording recommenced.

He heard a soft cough and worry sifted through his bones.

Gemma! What? Oh, no!

He frowned. *Wait. It's not like her to give herself away like that, is it? Not at all. She wouldn't draw attention to herself unless . . .*

Unless she meant to?

What he heard next was Cushing's oily, condescending voice. "Oh, dear, Dr. Prochanski. What have we here?"

Bickel endured more dead air until Prochanski spoke. "Gemma. *Gemma!*"

Another silence.

Then, "I'm sorry, Doctor. Did you need something?"

Bickel ground his teeth. "What in the world are you doing, Gemma?"

Apparently Cushing wondered the same thing. "What are you doing here, *Gemma?*"

Gemma, with passable innocence, replied, "Oh, I take the meeting minutes, ma'am, but I stopped taking them when Dr. Bickel left. Was that a mistake?"

Cushing's sickly-sweet voice asked, "Then what have you been doing the last few minutes, *Gemma?*"

When Gemma stuttered a bit, Bickel frowned. *What are you playing at, Gemma?*

But Gemma pushed on. "Nothing important, ma'am."

Bickel heard a sharp *snap*—Cushing snapping her fingers?

"Let me see."

Gemma whined, "Dr. P?"

Bickel's concern gave way to interest. *You don't stammer, and you don't whine. Curious.*

"Hand her your laptop, Gemma," Prochanski ordered. "Now."

Bickel heard nothing for about a minute; he assumed Gemma had handed over her laptop to Cushing.

When Cushing spoke again, all pretense of sweetness was gone. "What is this?" she demanded.

Prochanski backed her up. "Answer the general, Gemma."

After another moment, Gemma whispered, "It's Pinterest, ma'am."

"What is . . . *Pinterest?*" Cushing hissed.

Gemma stammered, and Bickel couldn't help himself. He grinned and barked a soft laugh.

Oh, you clever girl, you. I was right about you, wasn't I?

"I-I, it's, uh, like a picture-posting and sharing website. People create boards of what they're interested in, you know, stuff they like. I-I like history and like to collect black and white photographs. Those are, um, early images of New Mexico's Pueblo Indians. It's-it's a hobby."

Bickel envisioned Cushing's disgust, and he sniggered. *Nicely done, Miss Keyes!*

"Really, Dr. Prochanski. I'm surprised that you allow your employees to waste precious government resources on frivolous, non-work-related pursuits like this."

Prochanski replied, "I didn't think Sandia's IT settings allowed access to social media." He added, "I'm disappointed in you, Gemma."

Gemma's response, laden with pathos, pulled another chuckle from Bickel.

"I-I'm sorry, Dr. Prochanski. It won't happen again."

"You may go, Gemma."

"Thank you, sir."

The audio file ended with Gemma's footsteps as she left the conference room.

Well done, Gemma. An Oscar-worthy performance.

But Gemma's quick thinking didn't alleviate Bickel's anxiety for the young woman.

The problem, Gemma, is that you most certainly did hear too much. Did your little pretense convince Cushing and Prochanski that your attention was elsewhere? I doubt it. Besides . . . Cushing never leaves a loose end hanging, and you, my dear, are a loose end.

He closed his own laptop and lapsed into concerned thought.

What will they do to you, Gemma? And with all that I and my team are facing, how can I protect you? The corners of his mouth pulled down in dismay. *I don't know if there **is** anything I can do.*

He folded his hands and stared at his dry skin and the age spots to which fading gingers were prone. He sighed. Said quietly, "I don't know if you are listening. Don't know if you would do anything I asked of you . . . but this isn't for me, um, *God*. This is for *her*. Gemma doesn't deserve to be collateral damage in Cushing and Prochanski's heartless drive to steal my nanomites. Would you . . . would you please protect her?"

He left his office, walked to his lab, and worked himself without mercy until the end of the day. Much of what he did was on autopilot. His mind was preoccupied with the moving pieces he and his team would have to put into perfect, flawless motion to get him and the nanomites safely away. When he returned to his office at the end of the day, he glanced toward Gemma's cubicle.

She stood inside the countertop-height surround, immobile and unseeing. Until she noticed him. The sight of him jarred her from her haunted reflections.

Something has happened. Bickel closed his office door behind him, opened his laptop, connected to the bug on Gemma's laptop, and found another file to download. A file less than ten minutes old. He plugged in his earbuds and listened.

Prochanski's voice, calling from his office across the lobby from Bickel's office.

"Gemma, I need to speak with you."

He listened to her scuffling footsteps to Prochanski's door. Her settling into a chair.

Then, Prochanski's voice. "Gemma, I'm sorry to tell you this, but we are letting you go."

Bickel sucked in a breath. No wonder Gemma was thunderstruck. He found that he was outraged for her. *Those rats!* On the other hand, he was relieved. Prochanski wouldn't bother to fire her if he and Cushing felt the need to permanently silence her—or would they?

He listened to Gemma's response—this time genuine. Genuinely dumbfounded.

"I'm sorry? What do you mean?"

"The contract under which you were working has lost its funding, so your position here is terminated, I'm afraid. Effective immediately."

"I-I-I-you can't be serious? I'm sure the contract has enough money on it for two more years!"

Prochanski said nothing.

"Is it something I've done? It can't be that I was looking at Pinterest! Please let me fix this?"

"My dear Gemma, this is not a termination for cause. Your contract position has been eliminated. Budget cuts."

He paused and then added, "This topic will be covered in your exit interview, Gemma, but the policy is serious enough to bear reiteration: Everything you have read, seen ... and *heard* in your work here is classified and cannot be spoken of outside these walls. *To anyone.*"

Prochanski's emphasis on "heard" and "to anyone" was tainted with threat.

The file was silent for so long that Bickel wondered if it had ended. But no.

"I'll pack my things," Gemma said slowly. As if in a dream.

The lack of intonation spoke to her frame of mind: *devastated.*

"Very good, " Prochanski replied.

Bickel heard Prochanski pick up his phone.

"Please send security to conduct an exit interview and escort Ms. Keyes off base."

The audio file ended, leaving Bickel mentally scrambling. *That's what I saw her doing. Clearing out her desk.*

Then, *Oh! I need to retrieve the bug from Gemma's laptop right this minute—before Security arrives and removes the laptop.*

She was wiping down the surface of her workstation when he approached her cubicle's countertop.

"Gemma?"

"Yes?"

Yes, she was devastated.

"I, um, heard what happened, Gemma. I'm sorry."

Her eyes narrowed the slightest bit. Her reply was cool.

"Thank you."

She ignored him and continued putting things into a box, wiping the surface after she removed items.

"If you need a recommendation, I would be pleased to write one for you."

Surprise flittered across her face, but all she said for a second time was, "Thank you."

The officer from Sandia's security office came through the door, looked around, then moved toward Gemma's cubicle.

Bickel said, "Here's my card, Gemma. I've written my personal phone number and email address on it."

She nodded, distracted by the security officer's approach. When she turned toward the officer, Bickel leaned over the cubicle wall and dropped his business card on Gemma's desk. As he released it, he ran his finger across the back edge of her laptop where the network port was, slid a fingernail under the bug, popped it loose, and palmed it. Waited for Gemma to turn back to him.

He pointed. "I put my card there. Please take it with you."

Gemma again fixed him with a piercing appraisal. He didn't know who was more surprised—him or her—when she leaned toward him and whispered . . .

"Watch your back, Dr. Bickel."

⌘

BICKEL RETURNED TO his office and pondered his predicament. Gemma had been his unwitting eyes and ears into Prochanski's schemes. At this point, what would he do without her?

"Hmm."

Oh, that option comes with more risk, Bickel, he told himself.

His logical side yanked him up short. *The real risk is that if you don't act, you'll be blind to Prochanski's next moves!*

He waited until Prochanski left for the evening, locking his office door behind him.

Bickel removed a copy of the department's master key from his pocket and used it to gain entry to Prochanski's office. He retrieved a fresh black dot from his pocket, removed its adhesive backing, and planted it on the back edge of Prochanski's laptop. He added a second dot to the underside of Prochanski's desktop monitors.

And for good measure . . .

He left Prochanski's office, locking the door behind him, and entered the conference room. A portrait of the President hung on one of the conference room's walls. He planted a third bug on the top edge of the portrait's frame.

"That should do it."

⌘

THAT EVENING, HE recounted Prochanski and Cushing's conversation to his team.

Tony, ashen-faced, strummed his fingers on the table and bounced his foot—nervous cues not typical of him.

Rick couldn't stop shaking his head. "You're not joking?"

"I'd hardly joke about something as serious as murder, Rick."

Tony flinched. "And Gemma is gone? Prochanski fired her?"

Bickel nodded. "I overheard their exchange, Tony. I won't reveal my methods, but you should know that I took immediate steps to stay abreast of Prochanski and Cushing's plans in order to—shall we say— improve my odds of survival?"

His loyal techs, neither stupid nor obtuse, stared at him aghast, with expressions that may as well have been neon billboards flashing out their astonishment: *You did what? You bugged Prochanski's office?*

"Whatever happens next, I will do my best to protect you both. If, by chance you were to lose your jobs, I will make certain you find work elsewhere. You have my word," Bickel said.

"If and until that time comes, we must do *nothing* to let on that we know what Cushing and Prochanski are planning. We will carry on, cool and calm, until I remove the nanomites from the lab."

⌘⌘⌘⌘

CHAPTER 14

THE THIRD MONDAY in March, Bickel summoned his team to another emergency meeting at his house. That evening, they assembled around his dining table.

"What's up, Dr. B?" Tony asked, eyeing Bickel's solemn expression. "Gotta admit, I'm kind of spooked."

"Same," Rick said.

"It's not good news, I'm afraid. You both know about the upcoming demonstration, right? Supposedly, Cushing and Prochanski have arranged for a DOE bigwig and his entourage to visit the AMEMS department Wednesday. I am to provide an impressive dog-and-pony show."

"Supposedly, Doc?" Tony asked.

"Right. *Supposedly*. Like I said, I won't reveal my methods to you. Suffice it to say that I have incontrovertible proof that, in reality, there is no 'bigwig' and no demonstration, but the day remains guaranteed to end with a *bang*. Let me put it plainly: Cushing and Prochanski intend to get rid of the three of us."

"You're scaring me, Doc," Rick whispered.

"Good. Because if we don't act, by Wednesday afternoon, your wife will be a widow and your children fatherless. I'm not exaggerating."

Tony swallowed, then exhaled. "Do you know their plans?"

Bickel nodded. "Prochanski is going to blow up the lab. With us in it."

Rick shook his head. "Wow."

Tony said, "Yeah. Wow. The postdocs, too?"

"No, he will assign them work in the MEMS lab that day . . . to protect them."

Bickel's tone turned bitter. "The explosion is designed to make it look like *I* made a mistake, that it was *my* fault."

Tony asked, "What . . . what are we going to do?"

"Oh, we're going to let them detonate their little bomb. Just, shall we say, earlier than expected."

⌘

Wednesday unfolded with clockwork precision. The "demonstration" was scheduled for 1:00 p.m. in the AMEMS lab. Fifteen minutes prior, when Bickel and his techs would be setting up the experiment, Prochanski's explosives were supposed to detonate—but Bickel, with information obtained by listening in on Prochanski's conversations, searched for and located the device.

He reset the detonation time from 12:45 p.m. to 9:45 a.m., moving the explosion up three hours.

Shortly after 9:00 that morning, Prochanski made a show of coming into the lab and reading Bickel's lab notes. He glanced around and frowned.

"Where are your technicians, Dr. Bickel?"

"I sent Rick and Tony out on an errand. Don't worry—they'll be back in plenty of time."

Bickel started to turn away. "Oh, by the way. I came in early and skipped breakfast, so I'm headed to the café to grab something—if you don't mind."

"As you wish. As long as you are back at least a quarter hour before the demonstration starts."

Bickel nodded while he removed his lab coat. "You wanted to go over the presentation slides with me. I should be back in half an hour. I'll be pinched for time after that, but we can review the slides then, if that works for you?"

The idea that his slides needed Prochanski's review and approval grated on him, but it was the ploy Bickel needed to lure Prochanski into the lab at the right time.

"Fine. I'll be here."

Without overt haste, Bickel exited his lab a final time.

Outside the lab doors, he moved quickly down the stairs to the subbasement. There, in a closet, sat two ordinary-looking satchels or carryalls. The carryalls had rigid ports for flexible tubing and interiors lined with a polymer surface much cleaner than an operating room.

The day prior, with Rick keeping watch, Bickel had brought the satchels into the lab.

"Here's where our training pays off, Nano," he'd whispered.

He placed an ultrasonic signal device into each satchel, attached the specialized hosing to the satchels' ports, and hooked up the other ends of the hosing to identical ports in the 3D printer's housing where the nanomites "resided." Using a remote, he turned on both signal devices. After five minutes, he closed the ports on the satchels.

"I'm sorry to have divided your numbers, Nano. I realize you don't like it, but I promise all your members will rejoin the nanocloud presently."

He'd then removed the hosing from the printer, stashed it in another bag, picked up both carryalls, hastened down the stairs, and locked them in the closet.

That was yesterday. Today, he exited the building with the carryalls, got into his car, and drove away, heading toward the mountain.

Rick and Tony were waiting for him at the golf course in Rick's car. Bickel parked his car, grabbed the satchels, and climbed into Rick's passenger seat.

"Everything good, Dr. B?" Tony asked.

"Perfect. We should hurry, though. When the lab blows, the Air Force will lock down the base while they determine the threat level. You need to get off base before that happens."

It was the first time they'd gone through the PIDAS during daylight, and it felt odd. It was worse than odd when Rick pulled up to the bunker and it was time to say goodbye.

"Rick, I need you to write a note to the person who delivers our equipment orders to the storage unit.

"Let them know that we no longer need their services and leave a final payment—double the usual amount—for them. Then cancel our lease on the unit.

"Oh. And don't forget to pick up my car from the golf course parking lot and return it to the lab," Bickel said, his mind rushing ahead. "Then get off the base before the bomb goes off. If all goes according to plan, Prochanski will be dead, Cushing will, for a time, assume I died with him, and the two of you will be in the clear."

He cleared his throat. "Thank you, both of you. I . . . I cannot tell you how I appreciate—"

Emotions were running high, and they were awkwardly quiet. Then it was time.

"Have fun with your families on safari."

Rick nodded. "Right-o, Doc."

Tony stuck out his hand. "Best of luck, Dr. B. Can't wait until the day you introduce the nanomites to the world."

After Rick and Tony drove away, Bickel waited inside the bunker, the door cracked a couple of inches. Ten minutes passed. Fifteen. Twenty.

He listened until, in the distance, he heard a low rumble that grew louder. It was followed, seconds later, by a thunderous *boom*.

Goodbye, Dr. Blowhard.

Bickel closed and locked the bunker door, picked up his precious cargo, and headed for his lab under the mountain.

⌘⌘⌘⌘

PART 3:
THE UNFORESEEN ENDING

CHAPTER 15

BICKEL STIRRED HIS oatmeal, lost in rumination. He didn't notice when the spoon dropped into the bowl. He'd finished reading a rare communication from Tony, posted on an anonymous bulletin board.

Favorite hunting dog

found one dead bird

Will keep nose to ground

to pick up scent of second

June hotter than anticipated

Stay put and cool

I know I will

The interpretation was simple. *Cushing knows Prochanski died in that explosion—and I did not. She knows I'm alive, that I have the nanomites and she does not. And she's made life far too hot for Rick and Tony to attempt contact with me other than via the occasional cryptic post.*

He sighed. *I would feel guilt-ridden for life if anything injurious befell them or their families because of me.*

After nearly three months in solitude, Bickel often spoke aloud to himself. Oblivious to his actions, Bickel fished the spoon out of his oatmeal and said, "Cushing's surveillance takes Rick and Tony off the board entirely. But I need someone, a person on the outside—someone other than Rick or Tony, of course. Has to be an individual who's moderately intelligent, detail-oriented, and courageous, absolutely trustworthy . . . or, barring that, someone I can make financially dependent on me—enough to ensure their cooperation and compliance. And what else?"

Bickel leaned his elbow on the table and rested his chin on his hand. *It must be a person so far beneath Cushing's radar that Cushing wouldn't see him—even if he bumped into her on the street or spilled coffee into her lap! A mentally agile individual, able to think on his feet—*

quick to react, to adapt and innovate on the fly, to prevaricate convincingly if necessary.

But I know so few people here in Albuquerque—certainly no one who fits this bill.

He blinked. Sat up. His mouth opened, then snapped shut.

"Good heavens. I need Gemma Keyes."

⌘

MORE THAN A WEEK passed while Bickel considered and discarded various ways of reaching out to Gemma. His deliberations factored in Cushing herself, the threat she posed to him and, by extension, to the girl. He could not—for a single moment—forget that Cushing's paranoid suspicions and her quest for self-advancement were real . . . and funded by unknown actors within the deep pockets of the US Government.

Fact: Cushing could be monitoring Gemma. If so, Cushing's black-ops goons would have "eyes" on the girl's communications, her finances, her home. *Fact:* The method Bickel selected to contact Gemma had to reach her yet evade whatever surveillance Cushing might have in place.

He sniffed in derision. "Dear, *dear* Imogene. The time we spent as a couple was nothing if not informative. You taught me your character—*self-serving*—and your nature—*primal* and *vindictive*. You have kept track of me all these years, have monitored the progress of my research, have you? Guess what? I have followed your career also. Yes, I know what you are. I know, too, what they say about a leopard and his spots. I know you *too intimately* not to acknowledge the danger you pose."

He doodled on a pad, jotting down ideas, discarding some, keeping others.

"My approach to Gemma must appear innocuous in the sight of your vigilant jackboots, Imogene. Easily ignored. At the same time, my 'invitation' must snag Gemma's attention. Pique her curiosity."

Bickel had hacked the utility accounts of Kirtland Air Force Base, including the base's two Air Force wings, the many Air Force centers and offices, and the base's "tenants" such as Sandia Labs, DOE's National Training Center, and DOE's Office of Secure Transportation. He wrote code that spread his lab's power consumption across those hundreds of electrical accounts so that a "bump" in consumption within the mountain would not raise eyebrows.

So, was hacking Gemma Keyes' email and social media accounts difficult? No, performing a deep dive into Gemma's life was child's play. A walk in the park. A means to an end—that "end" being an accurate appraisal of Gemma's life and habits.

Tinkertoys, he laughed to himself.

He scrolled through her Gmail account, her social media profiles, credit reports, utilities, bank statements, and sources of income.

"Hmm. I see."

Bickel sat back and considered the picture her accounts, taken as a whole, painted of Miss Keyes. Rested his elbows on the table. Sorted through his bleak conclusions.

It bothered him that Gemma hadn't been able to find a job since Prochanski let her go. It bothered him a lot more that her sole source of income, unemployment, would expire soon. She had no savings. No partner or significant other. No close friends. Apparently, her sole living relative was a twin sister, an attorney in DC—and they didn't get on.

He shook his head. "You're broke and alone, Gemma. Four weeks longer and your bills will go unpaid. Two weeks later, they'll be past due. Even that old house your aunt left you has a mortgage on it."

He leaned back and stared up, his gaze tracing the cavern's domed ceiling. *What would it be like to have next to nothing, to live under straitened circumstances? No revenue, no substance, no unencumbered properties, no net worth to speak of. No one to catch you when you fall.*

Nodding to himself, he whispered, "Your luck is about to change, Gemma Keyes—that is, if I can contact you without attracting the Eye of Sauron. I think my plan can do that, but a lot depends on you, too. Will you notice and follow the trail of breadcrumbs I leave for you?"

He returned to Gemma's email account and studied her folders, focusing on her sent mail folder and her trash folder. When he felt that he'd acquired a good sense of the kind of emails she sent (mostly job applications) and the traffic her inbox saw on a regular basis (the usual spam and a demoralizing number of rejection letters) he decided to frame his methodology around them.

Eventually, he got to work. Building the pieces. Assembling the package.

"This had better work, Bickel," he warned himself. "You've got a lot riding on this little sortie."

Bickel spent three days patiently tweaking the bits and bytes until they suited his fastidious standards.

His message to her was the most delicate part. It had to be direct yet persuasive. Had to contain the right lure—the hook, so to speak. The message had to call on Gemma's sense of right and wrong, but it also had to intrigue her.

Despite your outward demeanor, you love the taste of a mystery. You relish a problem to be solved, don't you, Gemma? I must give you a puzzle you cannot ignore, one that will tease you until you bite.

When he finished the message, he encrypted it—but *lightly*. Titillating, but nothing a freeware decryption program couldn't crack. To the naked eye, the encrypted text would look like a remnant. The leftovers of a corrupt file. Of no consequence.

Gmail's spam filters would determine the success of his next step. Google's filters were good—and he was counting on them.

He opened a Hotmail account and composed an email to Gemma. Filled the email's subject field with *You'll Love My Photo*. Typed a single line of text in the body of the email: *Sorry for the spam.* Last, but entirely essential to his scheme, he attached an image to the email, an innocuous picture of Sandia Crest.

He laughed at the email as he sent it. "I'm writing Google a nasty review if Gemma's Gmail account doesn't consign you to her spam folder the second you hit their servers."

His ploy depended on it.

He navigated to Yahoo next and opened another email account. From that account, he composed an email to Gemma with a subject line that read *Re: Your Job Application.* As desperate for work as she was, she would hasten to open the email. When she did?

The body of *that* email also contained a single sentence: *Sorry for the spam.*

"If I know Gemma, she'll puzzle over that enigmatic statement. It will disrupt her sense of order. She'll wonder 'what spam?' and go looking for it, yes? And where does spam go to die? Why, the spam folder, of course."

He closed his eyes. *If Gemma is as bright as I deem her to be, she will open that folder and take a look—a careful, safe look, but a look just the same.*

Bickel chuckled. "She'll sort through the folder, ignoring the usual distasteful sales pitches, the ubiquitous calls to renew her auto warranty, the mendacious promises of rapid weight loss, and the polyglot pleas from all over the world for her to "renew" automobile warranty coverage she didn't own.

"But then she'll spy a unique header, *You'll Love My Photo*, and see no harm in opening the email—not clicking on links or attachments, of course. But when she does open the email, what will she see?

Sorry for the spam.

Again.

"And that's how I tweak your nose, Miss Keyes. Send you scampering back to your inbox to reread *Re: Your Job Application*. Yup. Two emails on the same day. Two unrelated senders. But the same message: *Sorry for the spam.*

He mused aloud, "She'll think the coincidence unlikely and will wonder, could it be . . . deliberate? The question will sit in the back of her mind like a tiny splinter, a sticker that irritates but cannot be removed. She'll take another look at the message Gmail sent to her spam folder. Compare the two emails side by side."

Bickel put himself in Gemma's seat and attempted to think and reason as she would: careful and cautious all the way.

*You aren't stupid, Gemma. You know that attachments or embedded links in emails from unknown senders are the universal red flags of malware. You know better than to open an attachment or click on a link without running a virus scan first—Computer Safety 101. And with a subject line like **You'll Love My Photo**, how could you **not** suspect porn—an open invitation for a ransomware invasion?*

*But, see, I know that **you** know how to run virus scans on email attachments. We did it regularly at Sandia with external emails. You know to move an attachment off your hard drive onto a flash drive first, then run a scan on the attachment. If—no, when—you scan the attachment and it comes back clean, will that overcome your caution?*

Will you dare to open the image?

"Yes, I trust you will, Gemma."

It wasn't that the picture itself was important, of course. What was important was the text file he'd embedded in the image—the message he'd composed to her. He had hidden the message as a zip file within the image's pixels.

There it waited for Gemma to find and decrypt it.

Bickel frowned and rubbed his weary features. He'd arrived at a sticking point—more than one. If Gemma did open the image, the harmless picture of Sandia Crest, would she simply shake her head, shrug, and throw it into the trash without a backward glance?

Or, would she think to examine the image for hidden data? Did she even have a passing knowledge of steganography and decryption? Or was she the dullard she pretended and not the bright young woman he judged her to be?

"I have faith in you, Gemma," he whispered. Then he chuckled.

"Oh, my dear Miss Keyes. You'll be completely surprised to find . . . that I'm alive."

He ran through the text of the letter once more—having unconsciously memorized it as he did so many things—this time reading it line by line as she would.

⌘

My Dear Miss Keyes,

If you are reading this message, then you truly are the intelligent, savvy young woman I took you for. For whatever reason, you have undervalued yourself and allowed others to do the same. But despite that remarkable, "flat" affect you habitually present to the world, I recognized that there was much more to you than you were willing to reveal.

As regards this message? I had to find a way to communicate with you, Miss Keyes, and it could not be out in the open. They are hunting for me, you see, and I could not take the chance that they might be monitoring you. Not that I think they are, mind you, but I could not risk it.

You see, you and the rest of the world think I'm dead. Unfortunately, Cushing knows better.

*Gemma (is it all right that I call you by your first name as we did at Sandia?), you were aware that I was doing advanced and classified R&D on the civilian side of things at Sandia. Dr. Prochanski liked to report on the state of "our" work, but the truth is that it was all me. I was doing the work; all the theories and efforts were **mine**. Dr. Prochanski may have* *led the AMEMS lab, but Sandia brought me in because **my** research in MEMS was years ahead of anything **his** puny mind could conceptualize.*

Dr. Prochanski, that underachieving braggart, couldn't grasp the progress I was making—not to mention the science behind it! I should say, "the progress I had made." Yes, I finally achieved the breakthrough I had theorized about and sought for most of my life. Decades of hard work, of dedicated research, design, and development paid off when I, ultimately, achieved my breakthrough goal.

Bickel paused. Muttered aloud. "I know, I know. I shouldn't brag."

Now I'm going to tell you why you lost your job—and why I had to "die."

*Dr. Prochanski had a secret deal with General Cushing—a secret deal he **thought** I knew nothing about. You see, I objected to any military appropriation or national security application of my work. Prochanski knew that and General Cushing knew that. They plotted to get my breakthrough to a prototype stage and then seize it for national security purposes—take it from the civilian side at Sandia to the military side.*

And they imagined I was at the "prototype" stage! Ha! They were the ones in the dark, despite Prochanski's efforts to monitor, record, and steal my work.

Gemma, while I worked at Sandia, I stayed aloof from everyone. As a person trying to hide my true agenda from Cushing and Prochanski, I couldn't help but notice you, to a degree, doing the same thing.

Yes, though you were an excellent member of the AMEMS team, you kept your little shield up all the time. I concluded that you had a need, as I had a need, to protect yourself. I don't say I understand your motives, but I recognized a kindred spirit in you . . .

He skipped ahead. *You must be wondering why I'm reaching out to you, Gemma. Here I must admit that I'm in a bit of a spot. To be plain, I need help and have no one in the immediate locale I can trust. Because we share a kindred spirit, I am willing to trust you. Will you trust me?*

I can't risk another email landing in your inbox. If you are afraid of getting involved, I won't blame you. Imogene Cushing is that scary. But if you are willing to take a chance or at least take another step, look for another piece of spam tomorrow.

Sincerely,

Daniel Bickel

PS: Delete this message and purge your email's trash folder.

⌘

BICKEL WAITED UNTIL late that evening to log into Gemma's Gmail account and check the status of *You'll Love My Photo*. If she'd opened the attachment, found the zip file, decrypted it, and read his letter, then the email would be gone—not merely deleted but purged along with the contents of her trash folder.

He could scarcely contain his glee when he clicked on the trash folder and found it empty. His shouts of joy echoed around the cavern's walls.

"You did it, you clever girl! You did it!"

⌘

LATER THAT NIGHT, Bickel composed his second email to Gemma, using the subject line *Don't Wait! Refi Now—Federally In$ured!*— yet another guaranteed delivery to her spam folder. After he sent the email, Bickel drummed his fingers on his desktop and allowed his mind to wander.

I wonder. Does Gemma hide her feelings in the privacy of her own home? Does she maintain her stoic countenance or is it only for public consumption?

He imagined her as she got up the following morning, opened her email, and clicked into her spam folder. Like his first email, he had attached an image to his second. No doubt, she would apply the same process to it as she had to his previous email's attachment—save it to a

113

flash drive and run it through a virus checker, then use steganography tools to reveal the hidden zip file and decrypt it.

Two items populated the zip file, a text file named "read_first" and a PDF file named "print_me." The text file was short and terse: *Print other and delete all.*

It was the printed PDF file that was most likely to freeze Gemma in her tracks and spell an end to Bickel's dreams.

The print job ran to three pages. Bickel placed copies of those pages on his desk and reexamined them. The first page was a rough map. The other two pages contained detailed directions with references to the map.

In his mind's eye, he saw her read the map, her sharp little mind soaking up its features, absorbing the minutiae, missing nothing. He imagined her reaction as she located the starting point indicated on the map . . . and after she traced the route to its termination point.

Bickel shivered. He had sent Gemma Rick's northern passage out of the mountain, but in reverse—a route that, according to Rick's assumptions, was to have been the President's emergency means of escape in time of war, should the enemy send an assault team into the mountain to breach the devolution site.

He traced the route himself . . . from the northeastern corner of the base's perimeter fence, south, then under the fence, across half a mile of base property, through the PIDAS surrounding the mountain, and up the mountain's slope to a set of tall rock pillars and the hidden door leading inside.

He swallowed hard. His heart pounded, and his restless fingertips came to a stop.

How will you react when you comprehend the magnitude of what I am asking of you, Miss Keyes?

⌘⌘⌘⌘

Chapter 16

BICKEL STEWED FOR three days. When would she come? Would she come at all? He feared the worst, because what he asked of her was presumptuous. Dangerous in more ways than one.

*I've asked Gemma, a young woman who owes me **nothing**, to shut down her phone so it can't be tracked—before she trespasses onto this base and makes an illegal trek up the side of the mountain. And that doesn't even touch the other instructions I sent her . . . how to locate and open the hidden door into the tunnels, how to find her way through the mountain's northern passage, the secret route that leads to this cavern.*

*If I were Gemma, would I do such a crazy thing? For **me**, practically a stranger?*

"Not on your life."

He paced and fretted, fretted and paced. He could not "switch off" his thoughts, as he envisioned and rationalized Gemma's response.

When his doubts grew too overwhelming, he told himself, "See, if Gemma is as inquisitive as I adjudge her to be, she will, at the least, attempt to debunk my instructions." Then he added, "She will think them the ravings of a madman, of course—but, being thorough, she will need to disprove those 'ravings' to her own satisfaction.

"So, at evening, tonight or tomorrow, she will park near the trailhead and, while pretending to hike the open space that runs alongside Kirtland's boundary, she will walk the base's perimeter fence, seeking my landmark."

He brightened momentarily. "She may be doing so already?"

Encouraged, he continued pacing. "She'll find the scrub piñon tree along the fence line right where it's indicated on the map. The tree's size and shape will match my description—thanks to Rick. And once she sees that the tree does indeed exist as I depicted, she'll find that its roots do grow down into an arroyo—also as my instructions told her."

He breathed in and out, in and out, his excitement growing. "Then comes the moment of decision. Will she crawl under the piñon tree's bushy branches, down into the arroyo's dry bed? When she spies where the earth has washed out under the base's fence—*as I told her*—will she wriggle under the fence? Will she go on from there?"

His scraggly brows drew down. "See, the thing I know about you, Gemma? You're all placid and innocent on the outside . . . but inside? You're an altogether different girl, filled with dreams and aspirations. And I know how angry you must be, angry that, through no fault of yours, you lost your job and can't find another one—dashing your ambitions to smithereens. You're likely blaming Cushing—and rightly so."

He sighed. "You would be right to be angry with me, too, Gemma. Yes, Prochanski used you, but I must admit that I did, too, something I regret."

His pacing slowed, and he bowed his chin to his chest. "If I have the opportunity, Gemma, I will do my best to make up to you what I've cost you. And yet, will your anger overcome your natural and understandable reticence, the fear of being caught trespassing on the base? Will your anger and your need for answers propel you up the mountain and into the tunnels?"

Bickel didn't have the chance to think further on his questions. From the back of the cavern he heard a soft scuffling. Fabric rubbing across rock. The sounds were unmistakable in the cavern's otherwise total silence: Someone on hands and knees was coming through the final bit of the low passage.

He stood frozen with anticipation.

A head lifted above the piles of furniture and looked around. A body followed, the head swiveling cautiously, scanning carefully.

When she edged toward his lab, he could wait no longer. "Hello, Gemma."

She turned toward him. "Hi, Dr. Bickel."

⌘

THEY WARMED TO each other gradually as Bickel showed her around his living quarters, then his lab. *His lab.* He tried to see it from her perspective and realized how underwhelming his setup had to appear—not much more than three rows of workbenches, computers, monitors, and equipment.

Nothing remarkable—nothing except the tall glass structure. Gemma wouldn't have the first clue what was inside of *it*.

He was dying to introduce her to the nanomites, but she wasn't ready to meet them. First she had to know how it was that he was *not* dead as the world believed . . . as Cushing and her people made certain they were told.

"They intended to eliminate me, Gemma."

"Kinda knew that, Dr. Bickel."

"Right. Of course you did. Well, I watched and listened carefully and learned their plan—to bomb my lab, with us in it."

He sobered. "It's good that you were so convincing that day in the conference room or Cushing might not have insisted that you be sent packing. She might have directed Prochanski to keep you around instead—then told him to send you on an errand into the lab when the 'accident' was scheduled to occur."

Except for the minute tightening of her mouth, Gemma's expression never changed. "So how did Dr. P end up dead and you, um, didn't? How did you escape?"

"Oh, yes. That. Prochanski and Cushing's plan was for Rick, Tony, and me to perish in their explosion. I learned both their timeline and their means."

He huffed. "I needed an exit strategy—better than the goodbye they had planned for me. So, when we uncovered their plot, we wrapped our plan around theirs. Unbeknownst to Prochanski and Cushing, I adjusted the detonation time on the device they'd planted. I moved it *up* three hours. I sent Rick and Tony on an errand off base before the real detonation time, leaving Prochanski and myself alone in the lab.

"I assured Prochanski that Rick and Tony would be back in plenty of time to set up for the 'demonstration.' Then, in that hour before the explosion, I told Prochanski I was stepping out for a short break. I left the lab long before the base was engulfed in chaos.

"When the device *did* detonate, Prochanski thought he had another three hours to get out and planned his movements accordingly."

Then Gemma did flinch. "But-but how did you get on and off the base? It was shut down for twenty-four hours. They searched every vehicle and person leaving the base for days. And your car was parked in the lot."

"I never left the base, Gemma. I never intended to. Rick and Tony took me to the mountain and returned my car to the lab parking lot. My car was found where Tony left it, but I've been *here* the whole time."

"Here? You've been here?"

"Yes."

"Uh . . . what is this place?"

Bickel grinned. "This, Gemma, is my notorious secret laboratory."

⌘

FOLLOWING HOURS OF explanations and demonstrations, they came back around to the reason Bickel had asked her to come to him.

"I need someone to be my liaison with the real world, Gemma. I own a safe house in Albuquerque—a residence I bought through a shell corporation. Untraceable, I assure you. The safe house is where we had the lab equipment sent when we were stocking this place.

"Occasionally I require parts or supplies for the lab, supplies that are vital to what I'm doing here. I can order what I need and have it sent to the safe house, but I need someone to pick up what I order and bring it to me."

"And?"

Bickel was embarrassed on the next point. "To be frank, I haven't had any fresh food since I went into hiding. The little frozen food I had is gone. All that remains is dried or canned. I-I need fresh meat, fruit, vegetables."

"You want me to grocery shop for you?"

He glanced down. "Three months without a steak, without a salad or an apple or yogurt is worse than I thought it would be."

"But . . ."

"But why *you*?"

"Yes. Why me, Dr. Bickel?"

"Because, dear Gemma, you don't have ties. People living with you, making demands on you, inquiring after your activities."

Her expression hardened. "What you mean is I don't have a family."

"I'm sorry, Gemma. I don't mean to wound you."

She *said* it was all right, but he could see he'd overstepped. Put his foot in it.

Plucking up her courage, she asked anyway, "What else?"

He nodded and looked down. "It occurred to me that you hadn't yet found suitable employment. And as you already knew what we were doing in the lab—at least in generalities—I hoped we might help each other. I will, of course, pay you well for your time. In cash."

"Most of all," Bickel added softly, "I selected you because I knew I could trust you. You see, I know you saw things you could have reported to Prochanski, but you didn't . . . and I believe we share a mutual, ah, *aversion* to General Cushing?"

"Her? I wouldn't believe her if she said my name was Gemma."

"Get in line! Imogene Cushing is intelligent, devious, and treacherous. She wants my work, Gemma, wants to take them—er, *it*—and use them—I mean *it*—to destroy every form of resistance to her twisted ideals of national security. Imogene Cushing views a police state as our nation's most secure defense."

"Obviously, you know her better than I do."

"Like I said, you are astute, Gemma. I met Imogene during our early days at Virginia Tech. She was ROTC then, and we were, once upon a time, er, close. She's an engineer—did you know that? And a superb strategist. When she graduated VT, she went into the Air Force as an officer and we . . . drifted apart."

Meaning she stole my paper and I broke it off with her!

"What I learned the hard way about Imogene is that, above all, she is ambitious. Ruthlessly, relentlessly ambitious. I made the mistake of sharing my dreams with her back then. She never forgot. She knew that I would someday make a contribution to science that would change the world, and she has dogged my career ever since—followed my research, read my publications, tracked my employment. It's no coincidence that she emerged on the scene just as my R&D came to fruition."

Dr. Bickel stared at Gemma. "I need to show you what I'm protecting here, Gemma. I need you to understand *why* General Cushing won't ever stop searching for me, why she had me declared dead after my body wasn't found in what was left of the AMEMS lab, and why I can never be seen in the open—at least not until I am ready. Until *they*— the nanomites—are ready and I have a means to keep them from being misused. Yes, I must show you!"

And so he did—although he tried to spare her the complexities of his design.

But I made a hash of it, he recalled afterward.

They did get through it—although Gemma displayed more spirit in their short conversation than he'd seen at any time while in the same department with her. She had interrupted him multiple times to ask questions. Had even put him in his place when his arrogance had, yet again, slipped out.

I deserved her rebuke, he admitted to himself. He even liked her better for it.

Finally, he offered her a midnight lunch. It was mere canned soup, but he'd made fresh bread to go with the soup. He'd watched her sniff the bread's yeasty freshness with pleasure.

"Please excuse this plain fare, Gemma," he apologized.

"But it's delicious, and this bread is wonderful. It's fresh, isn't it? Did you bake it yourself?"

He'd been inordinately pleased that she'd noticed. "I like to cook, but as I said, I have only dry and canned goods left. I hope the next time you come I might offer you something better."

"The next time?"

He swirled his spoon in his soup. "As I alluded to earlier, I asked you here to offer you a job, Gemma."

She set her spoon down. "I'm listening."

"Did you find the trek onto the base and up the foothills into the tunnels too rigorous?"

Too dangerous? Too scary?

She didn't answer right away, but she swallowed hard. "Not too."

"If you agree to my proposition, I would like you to make the trip on a regular basis, say once a week, bringing in things I need. I will pay you in cash for the items you bring me and pay you for each trip you make. What do you say?"

"I need time to think about it."

He perceived that the prospect terrified her, but he was hoping the money would make the difference.

At the end of the night, before dawn, Bickel counted out eight hundred dollars into Gemma's hand and gave her a list of items he wanted her to bring him in a week.

She fixed on the money, relief warring with trepidation and good sense.

With sudden clarity, Bickel knew she would come back.

⌘

AFTER GEMMA LEFT, Bickel sat for a long time, rehearsing her visit and their conversation. A wave of responsibility rolled over him.

I'm asking this young woman to put her life on the line. I'm placing her in Cushing's crosshairs.

He exhaled slowly. "You know I wouldn't want anything to happen to Gemma. I wouldn't ask her to come if completing the nanomites' training wasn't so pressing, if I didn't need the bits of equipment she will bring me. So please . . . God. Please keep her safe."

Nodding, he added, "Thank you and, er, amen? Yes. Amen."

⌘⌘⌘⌘

CHAPTER 17

GEMMA RETURNED THE following week, bringing Bickel joy in the form of fresh meat and produce. He was thrilled. He found, to his surprise, that he was also grateful for the young woman's company.

Not that they didn't knock heads more than once. What he hadn't expected was for Gemma to assert herself—and not back down.

*Why, she thinks **she** has the upper hand!* he was shocked to realize.

In a way she did. But as they worked out the details of their arrangement, it became obvious that they each had what the other needed and the leverage that went with it. So, they found ways to compromise.

Gemma began to arrive weekly. She crawled or duck-walked her way out of the narrow entry point at the back of the cavern, dragging his supplies behind her. During her visits, she taught him a complex card game that used three decks, and brought with her a taste of human kindness and companionship he desperately needed. He responded by cooking for her. Anything to lengthen her stay.

Gemma made the trek into the mountain through July and August. Right up to the midpoint of September.

That was when Cushing caught up with them.

⌘

BICKEL GRINNED AS he served the day's festive lunch—bowls of pasta and pesto sauce strewn with artichoke hearts and tender bites of chicken, a nice salad on the side, accompanied by fresh-baked garlic bread.

Gemma attacked her meal with the gusto of youth and praised his cooking to the skies. Bickel soaked up her compliments like dry earth soaks up rain.

After they finished eating, he brought out the desserts and sketched a mock bow over them. His treats were simple today—frozen fruit parfaits in tall glasses—but the glasses gleamed with colorful sliced fruits and flavored ices. Sweet and pleasing to the eye.

"Oh, they're gorgeous! But I'm too full to eat another bite right now," Gemma moaned, holding her stomach. She powered on her phone, snapped a picture of the parfaits, and shut down the phone after.

"Let's save them for later. Please?"

"Right you are," he concurred. "I'll put them back in the freezer."

"And I'll deal the cards."

"Beware, Gemma! I'm going to beat you today," Bickel tossed over his shoulder from the little kitchen.

She cackled a devious laugh. "Sure, pal! We'll see about that."

Bickel smiled to himself as he closed the freezer door. *I knew there was more to this girl the moment I laid eyes on her—her and that "watch me vanish into the wallpaper" routine. I might not know the source of her fear and caution, and maybe I can't understand why she keeps the real Gemma so carefully hidden away, but I do know this: She truly is the proverbial diamond in the rough.*

He paused as a deep realization struck him. *I also know that I might have cracked up by now without her assistance . . . no, without her friendship. How dear she has grown to my heart!*

An unexpected, a *foreign* possibility crossed his mind. Instead of pushing it away, he forced himself to examine it. *Was it you? Did you bring Gemma to me . . . God?*

He stalled out on the question. Nearly choked on the years of guilty feelings he'd kept carefully locked away.

*I, uh, haven't paid much attention to you lately—not for ages, if I'm honest with myself or, rather, honest with **you**. And for a change, I can't pull out the excuse that I've been too busy, too pressured by my work— not in the months I've been hiding here inside this mountain.*

He expected to sense an angry rebuke or, more likely, outright rejection, but . . .

His brows shot up, then his features collapsed into quizzical lines. *What is this? What am I feeling?*

A weight lifting from his shoulders? Something—some*one*—tugging at him, urging and drawing him?

The burden of guilt he carried in his heart, a heaviness familiar enough for him to think it *normal*, seeped away. In its place he felt something different. What was it? Was it gentleness? Kindness? Encouragement? Was it . . . love?

He swallowed convulsively. *I'd like things to change between us, Jesus. That is, if that's something you want, too. If you're willing to forgive me.*

He was surprised to hear himself whisper, "Jesus, would you please forgive me?"

He sensed no cosmic shift and heard no audible voice in response. Nevertheless, a hopeful little candle within him flickered to life. It was a start, and he exhaled. Smiled.

"Thank you."

He was smiling when he sat down opposite Gemma and they began to play.

Play? Oh, they "played" all right. They played to win and entered each battle with barely-this-side-of-civilized rivalry. Yes, he'd grown to appreciate their friendly warfare as much as she did.

She crooked one brow at him. "What?"

He cleared his throat. "Nothing. I . . . I'm glad you're here, Gemma."

She grinned. "Me, too, Dr. Bickel."

Less than five minutes later, she laid down her hand and crowed, "I'm out!"

Bickel growled. "You caught me with six hundred points in my hand!"

She laughed as she counted up her bonus points, then toted up the scores. "I'm up by 1,500!"

The game took 10,000 points to win, so Bickel wasn't worried—not yet. He shuffled and dealt the next hand. As he picked up his hand and started sorting his cards, he said, "Don't count me out, Gemma. I'll catch you this time."

"Ha! Sure you will!"

Bickel blinked. Something had disturbed his concentration. A distant tremor. The slightest rumble. A vibration in his chest.

⌘⌘⌘⌘

CHAPTER 18

DR. BICKEL'S CHIN jerked up. His eyes darted about the cavern, seeking the source of his concern.

What is it? What—

The events that followed were packed so tightly together as to be nearly concurrent: A tremendous explosion rocked him, followed by a sucking vacuum that stole the air from his lungs. The atmosphere within the cavern seemed to expand and roll over him. It squeezed his body until his chest and ears were near to bursting. The roiling pressure tossed Bickel and Gemma from their seats and slammed them to the stone floor.

Dirt and pieces of rock cascaded from the cavern's ceiling and pelted them. Bickel coughed and choked on the dust-clogged air. He tried to move, tried to get up off the floor, but he couldn't get his brain to send the right signals to his legs—and it was vital that he move quickly.

Cushing. Her jackboots are coming through the construction tunnel! She's blasting through the decoys and diversions!

He forced a single, grunted word from his mouth. "Gemma."

It was no louder than a whisper.

He commanded his mind to shake off its confusion. Coughed to clear his throat. "Gemma! They're blasting through, Gemma! We don't have much time!"

Gemma, her expression dazed, struggled to sit up. "What do you need me to do?"

Bickel shifted his vision toward his lab. Toward the glass case. His life's work.

Right then, the lights encircling the cavern's ceiling flickered and died. Battery-powered emergency lights began to glow dimly around the cavern. At the same time, from the decoy tunnel, came a thundering *thump-thump-thump* that bespoke Cushing's determination to gain access to the old devolution site.

Bickel's thoughts ran wild, tripping over each other.

I modified the decoy route to delay Cushing, to slow her down. I planted false turns and dead ends along the passageway to obstruct and hinder her goons, to keep them from breaching the cavern too quickly. To give me time. Time to escape. What must I do first?

He already knew the answer; he had reflected on this scenario countless times. *She must not get her hands on the nanomites! Even if the nanomites should die, their deaths would be preferable to Cushing taking possession of them, but—*

A different priority slapped him—one he had *not* planned for—and that priority was like a second train on the same track as his escape plan—the two engines headed at full speed toward each other.

Gemma! She is innocent, and Cushing knows nothing of her. I must get her out of here before Cushing breaks through!

His careful deliberations collided and tangled into a fruitless snarl. His mind spun in futile motion until his analytical side asserted itself and reordered his priorities.

*Look, Bickel, you have several minutes before Cushing's storm troopers gain entry, not enough time to save Gemma, the nanomites, **and** you—but Gemma must be your first concern. Instead of trying to remove the nanomites and escape with them, you may need to release the nanocloud into the cavern. Cushing could stand right under them and never find them.*

He answered himself. *But if I release the nanomites from their case and separate them from their source of power, they will probably flounder and die.*

His analytical side retorted, *It is the price you may have to pay, because you cannot allow the nanomites or your notes to fall into Cushing's hands.*

"Nor can I allow Cushing to capture Gemma," he whispered.

A course of action rushed into his head. *Cushing is ignorant of Gemma's presence here or the help she's given me, and Cushing also doesn't know about the exit at the back of the cavern.*

Send Gemma out the back entrance ASAP! He nodded to himself. *I will pack up the nanomites and have her take them and my notes out with her. As for me? I've had a good run.*

He hesitated. *Lord? Will you receive me? In spite of all my failings?*

He pushed himself up and sprinted toward his lab, toward the nanomites, Gemma stumbling along behind him.

"Gemma. My most recent lab book is over by the microscopes. Get the book and any stray notes I've left lying around. Get them. Quickly!"

"Yes, Dr. Bickel."

She veered off toward the lab tables; he raced toward the transparent glass case. Beneath the case, within the cupboard, were the two carryalls he'd used to bring the nanomites into the mountain. He dragged them out, his mind flying through his options, weighing them, choosing those he hoped would work.

Get the nanomites to flow back into the carryalls. Send Gemma out the way she came in—with the carryalls and my notes. She will escape and give the mites a chance to survive. God willing, they will find a way.

The cavern shook with another explosion as Gemma arrived with his lab book and a handful of stray pages. Bickel grabbed at a table edge to keep from falling. Gemma shook herself and waited quietly as he connected the white, flexible tubing to a rigid port in the first bag's side.

"Don't worry, dear girl. The nanomites will flow back into the carryalls," he shouted. "As soon as they are inside, take them and go. I'll be right behind you."

He didn't say aloud what he added silently: *if God grants me such a mercy.*

He had clamped the tube onto the second carryall's port when yet another blast rumbled into the cavern. It knocked both of them backward. Gemma clutched at her ears and keened as the change of pressure pained them. Larger chunks of rock fell on the lab and demolished precious equipment. Bickel turned at a low moan from Gemma and saw blood oozing from her head.

No! I cannot afford another distraction! he told himself. *They are blowing through the decoys quicker than I had judged possible. How much time do I have left?*

Dr. Bickel grabbed the edge of the nearest lab table, pulled himself to his feet, dropped the tubing, and ran toward the front of the lab. From there he had an unobstructed view of where the decoy tunnel emptied into the cavern.

Dust flowed from it—dust and the indistinct sounds of muffled voices.

Reality hit him hard. *I can save Gemma—get her out of here before Cushing's men arrive—but not if she waits for the nanomites to enter the carryalls. I cannot save them. I can only release them and trust for the best.*

He rushed back to Gemma and shouted, "Cushing's men are coming through, Gemma! Soldiers. Lots of them. My delaying tactics didn't slow them down long enough."

She stared stupidly at him, but she had his lab book. Good.

"I need you to go, Gemma. Quickly."

"You, too, Dr. Bickel," she replied. "You're coming, too—right?"

"Yes, yes. I'll be right there. Now, go! Get out now!" He gave her a little shove toward the back of the cavern.

With Gemma safely out of harm's way, he could manage this last task. He bent and yanked another object from the cabinet below the glass case. When he stood up he wielded the aluminum baseball bat he'd placed there.

I never wanted to need this.

He hefted the bat, drew it back over his shoulder, and slammed it forward onto a corner of the glass case. To his dismay, it rebounded!

"Dr. Bickel! Hurry!"

"Yes, yes! Go, Gemma!"

Shouts echoed from far down the decoy tunnel. The intruders were through! They would be in the cavern itself in moments.

Fear jarred him from his daze.

He swung the bat once more, and the case's corner seam split apart. Instantly the air buzzed with an unnatural hum.

"Hide!" Dr. Bickel shouted to the nanomites. Red-faced, he waved his arms in the air. *"Nano! Hide!"*

Hide. He had trained them to that one-word command. He watched the swarm as it left the case. They poured like vapor from the wide-open seam. Once clear of the glass, they gathered themselves into a dense ball and shot into the air, a shimmering silver-blue haze . . . that vanished.

The tramp of boots and shouted orders drew closer.

"Thank God," Dr. Bickel said aloud. He whirled around—and stopped short.

"No! Gemma, what are you doing here? I told you to go!"

When she didn't move, he shoved her in the direction of the cavern's back wall, and shrieked. "Go! Before they see you, Gemma!"

She finally turned and stumbled toward the rear of the cavern.

He watched her go, knowing that the soldiers would round the perimeter of the lab tables any moment, that Gemma needed to reach the piled-up office furnishings to be hidden from their sight but—

What is she doing? No!

Gemma slowed and glanced behind her. Then she halted and looked back. Motioned to him. "Dr. Bickel! Hurry!"

Bickel knew he had but seconds. Once the soldiers reached him, they would see her. He bellowed as loud as he could, "Hide! Hide, Gemma!"

What?

He blinked stupidly and slowly, uncertain of what he saw. Gemma jerked. Her back bowed as though she were starting a back bend. Her arms flew up over her head. Her entire body momentarily left the ground as though something heavy, something *with force behind it,* had struck her between her shoulder blades, bent her, lifted her into the air.

Then it was over. She dropped to her knees and collapsed onto her face.

Boots pounded on stone, and Bickel turned. A dozen men in black tactical gear raced toward him. The black-garbed men opened fire.

Bickel felt multiple rounds strike his chest before he heard the shots echo through the cavern. He cried out in agony as ribs broke and flesh tore. The force of impact spun him around.

Suddenly he could not breathe. His knees buckled. He fell slowly, as if from a great height, his vision narrowing around the edges.

The cold stone floor reached up to gather him into its embrace. He felt its chill begin to seep into his body, into his bones. His cheek came to rest on one outflung arm.

He had but one consideration: *Gemma!*

He forced his eyes open; he looked for her but could not find her. *No—there she is!*

She lay face down on the rock floor. Unmoving. Quiescent. Lifeless? Yet, while he watched, her body twitched. The way it jostled was . . . odd.

He blinked to clear his vision. *What is happening?*

The "middle" of her prostrate form rose from the stone floor looking remarkably like—and the similarity disturbed him—a human inchworm . . . except that both of her arms and hands hung limp from her shoulders, *not* pushing her up. A physiological impossibility!

In that bizarre manner, Gemma dragged herself toward the exit hidden by the rock overhang. Closer and closer. Almost there.

Would she make it? Would she escape unseen? What about the nanomites?

"Gemma." Nothing emerged from between his lips. "Gemma!" He shouted, but the word was without sound, and he could not draw another full breath.

Gemma! Lord, please protect her!

Cushing's soldiers had not yet reached him, but that also meant they couldn't see Gemma.

*And if the soldiers couldn't see Gemma from the front of the cavern, they could not have shot her . . . could they? But if **they** didn't shoot her, then who did?*

His mind struggled to understand, to make sense of what he'd witnessed, yet he was finding it difficult to hold on to his thoughts. The cold of the stones beneath him was seeping into his body, chilling his flesh, numbing his senses. His emotions flickered wildly between despair and anxious petition.

Am I dying? Is this my ignoble end? But what about Gemma? She doesn't deserve my fate. Please! Will you help her make it out alive?

Drawing a painful, shuddering breath, he attempted to lift his head and crack open one eye. His head lolled back a few inches, but all he saw was gray fog, edging nearer. He squinted and pushed back on the encroaching darkness.

He needed one final glimpse of the young woman! One!

Please, Lord God—I want to see Gemma make it into the tunnels. To know she is safe.

Through the haze closing in on him, the movement of her body snagged his attention.

What in the world?

Through bleary, unfocused eyes, he watched a strange, impossible sight: Gemma's prostrate form, head and shoulders first, disappearing inches at a time into the space beneath the overhang—as if she were being towed into that low, narrow passage leading to the tunnels.

Towed?

Or *tugged?*

The answer hit him like a sledgehammer. *The nanomites!* They were pulling her!

Gemma's torso, legs, and feet shimmered suddenly with silver-blue haze . . . *and vanished.*

Bickel gasped. Gemma was gone! Gone the same way the nano-mites had hidden themselves at Bickel's one-word command: "Hide, Nano!"

He swallowed with difficulty and replayed what he'd seen.

But it can't be! That would be impossible, yes?

Unless . . . unless the nanomites had responded to his frantic, "Hide! Hide, Gemma!" Could the nanomites have taken his words as a command *they* were to carry out?

Unlikely and improbable, certainly! Yet nothing else explained what he'd witnessed. And what did it matter so long as Gemma was safe?

A flood of relief flowed over him. *You heard me, Lord God, and oh! How I thank you!*

He sucked in another tortured breath.

*Dear, **dear** Gemma! The Lord protect and keep you—keep you safe from Cushing's clutches.*

This is your story now.

He exhaled.

Allowed himself to let go.

The End

⌘⌘⌘⌘

Follow your read of **Stealth Genesis** with
Stealthy Steps, Book 1 in the Nanostealth series
. . . where the action *really* begins!

STEALTHY STEPS

VIKKI KESTELL

NANOSTEALTH BOOK 1

Faith-Filled Fiction™

www.faith-filledfiction.com | www.vikkikestell.com

And now . . .

The Christian and The Vampire—A Short Story

Vikki Kestell
The Christian and the Vampire
a short story
Faith-Filled Fiction™
www.faith filledfiction.com | www.vikkikestell.com

THE CHRISTIAN AND THE VAMPIRE
A Short Story
Also Available in eBook Format

BOOKS BY VIKKI KESTELL

NANOSTEALTH

Book 1: *Stealthy Steps*
Book 2: *Stealth Power*
Book 3: *Stealth Retribution*
Book 4: *Deep State Stealth*, 2019 Selah Award Winner
Book 5: *Stealth Insurgence*
Book 6: *Stealth Triumph*
Stealth Genesis, a Nanostealth Prequel

A PRAIRIE HERITAGE

Book 1: *A Rose Blooms Twice*
Book 2: *Wild Heart on the Prairie*
Book 3: *Joy on This Mountain*
Book 4: *The Captive Within*
Book 5: *Stolen*
Book 6: *Lost Are Found*
Book 7: *All God's Promises*
Book 8: *The Heart of Joy—A Short Story*
Book 9: *Rose of RiverBend*

GIRLS FROM THE MOUNTAIN

Book 1: *Tabitha*
Book 2: *Tory*
Book 3: *Sarah Redeemed*

LAYNIE PORTLAND

Book 1: *Laynie Portland, Spy Rising—The Prequel*
Book 2: *Laynie Portland, Retired Spy*
Book 3: *Laynie Portland, Renegade Spy*
Book 4: *Laynie Portland, Spy Resurrected*

STEALTH GENESIS WITH BONUS CONTENT,
THE CHRISTIAN AND THE VAMPIRE—A SHORT STORY
Copyright ©2022 Vikki Kestell
ISBN-13: 978-1-970120-33-2
ISBN-10: 1-970120-33-9

THE CHRISTIAN AND THE VAMPIRE
A Short Story
Copyright ©2014, ©2022 Vikki Kestell
All Rights Reserved
Also Available in eBook Format

What happens one sultry summer night when a Christian and a vampire meet on a fire escape and agree to engage in a cordial conversation? A touch of hilarity, plus eye-popping—and Undead *heart-starting*—revelation as vampire myths and legends give way to greater Truth!

SCRIPTURE QUOTATIONS

King James Version (KJV)
Public Domain.

⌘

New English Translation (NET)
Scripture quoted by permission.
Quotations designated (NET)
are from the NET Bible® copyright ©1996-2006
by Biblical Studies Press, L.L.C.
http://netbible.com
All rights reserved.

⌘

The New International Version (NIV)
The HOLY BIBLE,
NEW INTERNATIONAL VERSION®.
Copyright © 1973, 1978, 1984
International Bible Society.
Used by permission of Zondervan.
All rights reserved.

⌘

New Living Translation (NLT)
Holy Bible. New Living Translation
copyright© 1996, 2004, 2007 by
Tyndale House Foundation.
Used by permission
of **Tyndale House Publishers Inc.,**
Carol Stream, Illinois 60188.
All rights reserved.

⌘

New King James Version® (NKJV®)
Scripture taken from the New King James Version.
Copyright © 1982 by Thomas Nelson, Inc.
Used by permission. All rights reserved.

FAITH-FILLED FICTION

http://www.faith-filledfiction.com/
http://www.vikkikestell.com/

⌘

ACKNOWLEDGEMENTS

My thanks to **Cheryl Adkins**
for her proofreading and enthusiasm for this project!

⌘

CHAPTER 1

Behold, I send you forth as sheep in the midst of wolves:
be ye therefore wise as serpents, and harmless as doves.
Matthew 10:16, KJV

MY *SPIDEY-SENSE* leapt into high alert.

We were down in The Glades passing out little books about Jesus—thin, pocket-sized graphic novels with titles like *Ridiculous Truths* and *Blood Sacrifice*. The Glades is where the local goths and vampire wannabes hang out—exactly the ones we were there to bring our message to. Hence the graphic novels.

We'd had a pretty good night, Jake and I. We'd passed out lots of the books, engaged in some decent conversation, and even prayed with one guy. I was pretty sure we would see him again.

What city?

Well, does it matter?

You could call it Gotham and that would be an apt characterization of our city: Lots of dark corners, pervasive decay, and evil doings.

And The Glades? Also a suitable metaphor. If you know *Arrow* you snapped to the reference and I don't need to explain further.

What I'm saying is that I'm not going to draw a *map* to this city and, in particular, this moldering urban hellhole, because as sure as I'm penning my memoirs of this encounter, some nit who has *no* business attempting a conversation with an Undead will pull a "Seven Sons of Sceva" and find out too late the truth of Acts 19:13-16.

So. Back to the story.

My *spidey-sense* leapt into high alert.

You know: The hair on the back of my neck standing at attention.

The skin on my arms scrambling up in cold gooseflesh.

Instant hyper-vigilance.

Just as an aside: if I were recording this uncommon *tête-à-tête* for "church folks" I might have written, "my spiritual discernment alerted me" or "the Holy Spirit spoke to me," but I'm not penning this tale for the benefit of those who are already God-followers. Nope. This account is for those to whom "spidey-sense" makes "perfect sense."

A chill traveled (literally) down my back, and I froze in place, scanning the area, not that I could see all that much. Jake and I had stopped at the mouth of a particularly dim and disgusting alley. It smelled rank and looked worse. We knew we'd find a clutch of Dead Beats (Undead posers) far down the alley's gaping maw, engaged in God-knows-what perverse activities.

The posers were (predictably) young men and women dressed or draped all in black, accented with deep purples and scarlet, with skin painted pale-to-white, hair dyed black, excessive black eyeliner, black lipstick, black manicures, and extreme piercings—you get the picture. Oh. And either nicely sharpened fangs that slip over their real teeth or (for the True Believers) permanently attached custom veneers or implants.

So here we stood, Jake and I, backs pressed against a seeping brick wall on the edge of a badly lit street, and something was, for certain, not right. I mean "not right" in addition to all the other aforementioned stuff.

Me, I'd done a stretch in the Marines, including two tours in the Persian Gulf, and I know what it is to be afraid. I'd seen things—awful things I'd like to forget—but I'd also seen what I believe is the most terrifying thing of all: a soul departing this life with no hope for a happy eternity.

Now *that's* terrifying. #aintnosecondchancesafterdeath

I suppose that's why, when I mustered out, I went off to Bible school. These days I hire myself out for day labor and spend most evenings down here in The Glades. The Glades, where "terrifying" is supposed to be "cool" but they haven't got a clue. Not yet, anyway.

So I'm looking around, checking my six, and seeing nothing—which is a lot worse than seeing "something" when you can sense that "something" is lurking close by. It's like spotting a spider in the shower (always, *of course*, while you're buck *naked* in the shower), turning around to grab a piece of TP and, when you turn back to squash the little beggar, he's gone.

You know he's still lurking somewhere nearby . . . but you can't find him. And that's not cool.

"What's up, Taz?" Jake whispered.

"Dunno, but I can feel it."

"You wanna get out of here?"

"Maybe. Hang on a tick."

Taz is the nickname I earned in the Corps. Short for Tasmanian Devil. Why? They said I didn't quit. That I just kept whirling. Kept fighting. Well, if the choice is fight or die, Imma gonna fight and not quit.

Whatever. The name stuck. Even had a Warner Bros. version of the Tasmanian Devil inked on my proud black skin. Now my nickname feels natural. But for different reasons. Spiritual reasons.

I knew that whatever "it" was, it still lurked close by. But I also recognized that Jake was new to spiritual warfare[1], so I gave in.

"Yeah. Let's call it a night."

I had the strong sense that, for me, though, the night wasn't over, so I muttered a quick, "You know I'm leaning on you, Jesus, right? I place my trust in you."

Then we bugged outta there.

A Ω

---

[1] For though we live in the world, we do not wage war as the world does. The weapons we fight with are not the weapons of the world. On the contrary, they have divine power to demolish strongholds. We demolish arguments and every pretension that sets itself up against the knowledge of God, and we take captive every thought to make it obedient to Christ. —2 Corinthians 10:3-5, NIV

CHAPTER 2

MY WALKUP STUDIO apartment isn't any great shakes, but it's mine and it's pretty secure, given the crime-riddled area I live in. I say it's I secure because of the reinforced door with deadbolts and the single window with locking bars across it. The bars are fairly strong: Ain't nothin' bigger'n a rat comin' through that window.

Nothing physical, that is.

That night I stepped through the door and ran the "I just got home" drill: Check the door and the lock for scratches or scrapes. Get inside and scan the single room for disturbances, even minor ones. Lock the door behind me. Check that the window is still intact and latched; unlatch and open the window; check that the exterior bars are still locked.

Relax.

I left the window open hoping for some fresher air. Then I threw some ripe fruit and OJ into the blender with a fistful of ice cubes and let them grind and whirr for 30 seconds. Poured the concoction out into a tall glass, unlocked the window bars, and stepped out onto the fire escape where I could look down on the street.

Hey, the view from the fire escape is the only view I've got and I've come to appreciate it. Besides, the apartment is always unbearable on a hot summer night, and hanging out on the fire escape is way cooler.

I tossed back half of the smoothie. The icy sludge tasted good but gave me instant brain freeze. Argh! Hate that.

Down on the street traffic was sporadic: Late nights during the week, the city took a deep breath, held it for a couple of hours, and let it go about four a.m. Then it was time to get up and climb aboard the hamster wheel once again.

That's when I sensed his presence but took a deliberate slug of the smoothie before I said anything. I didn't turn around.

"I was wondering if you'd show yourself," I opened in a conversational tone.

"And here *I* was wondering how badly my presence would upset you."

I have to give props where they're owed. The dude's voice could melt ice down to a puddle in seconds. It was mellow, rich, and liquid gold. Seductive. Mesmerizing.

I took another slug of my smoothie, then upended the glass and let the remains dribble into my mouth. "Hate how the strawberry seeds all sink to the bottom of the glass, don't you? Last mouthful is just full of 'em." I turned around and plunked the empty glass on the window ledge.

"Hey. I'm Taz."

He was hardly more than the shadows where the fire escape steps butted up against the grimy outside of my apartment. For the moment.

I caught the flash of bright white as he smiled. "Ah, yes. I know your name, of course." His words were molten charm sprinkled with a dash of good-natured sarcasm.

"Well, I like to start off polite and all," I remarked.

He smiled again, that glint of his teeth, and then I could make out his shape a bit more. He spread his hands. "Forgive me. You may call me . . . Lambros, Taz."

"Lambros. As in the Greek word for *brilliant*? Interesting. Does it refer to your intellect or your shiny appearance?"

Okay; I admit I sometimes have a smart mouth.

His outline was, bit by bit, coming into focus. Now I could tell that he was tall and lean, but he kept his face in the shadows. He didn't answer my smart-alecky question.

"So what can I do for you, Lambros?" I inquired.

"Oh, I'm just in the mood for some good conversation. *Cordial* conversation, I assure you." The shadows twisted and I thought he turned toward me. "What do you say, Taz?"

"I can always agree to a cordial conversation."

"Ah. Good."

I saw that flash of white again and the faint outline of a sharp jaw. His voice was young and cultured, and I guessed his age at about thirty, but . . . but his elegant manner belied that relatively youthful age. Something distinctly *mature*, old-fashioned even, emanated from him, and I warned myself not to base my estimation of his age on his appearance.

"I watched you work down in the Glades tonight," he murmured, "and I confess I am somewhat *curious* . . . about you . . . Taz."

He paused before adding, casually, "Dear me. This rusty old fire escape doesn't lend itself much to comfort or civility, does it? Might we be more at our ease inside?"

"You want me to invite a vampire into my home." I waggled my eyebrows and just looked at him. Like, *really*?

He giggled low in his throat, tickled that I'd found him out so quickly. "But surely you're not afraid?"

I shrugged. "Not afraid. Just not stupid."

He spread his hands again, a self-deprecating gesture. "It was just a . . . *cordial* suggestion, Taz."

"Well, could I offer you something to drink?" *I* smiled this time. "In the spirit of cordiality, of course."

It was quite interesting how his eyes flared red. I hadn't been 100 percent certain where they were until they did.

Annnnnd apparently I'd ticked him off.

Α Ω

CHAPTER 3

"Do you think you could get through that window before I was on you?" he threatened, his shadowy form easing toward me.

"No." My response was matter-of-fact, accompanied by a shrug. "But you wouldn't like how I taste. Blood of *Jesus* and all."

He flinched at The Name and drew back, retreating to the corner. His form rippled and again mingled with the shadows. Watching how he shapeshifted reminded me of how a flock of birds will lift off, their swarm swirling in outline and size, then return to settle in much the same place.

I kept quiet and kept watching. I wasn't surprised that he'd pulled back when I'd said The Name, but I *was* surprised that he stuck around.

Why? I asked myself. *What does he want?*

Anyway, after a few minutes I think we both settled down, so I pushed our convo in a calmer direction. "You said you'd been watching us work down in The Glades. Said you were curious." He didn't answer immediately, and I wondered if he'd just eventually depart without further word.

He and I were, I mused as I waited, on a somewhat-comparable plane: me with my smooth, black skin as nearly invisible in the inky darkness as he was. And by the way, he wasn't the only one on that fire escape with pearly whites that could gleam in the night.

Similarities and differences aside, I might be a proud Marine and a proud black American, but it wasn't my skills or pride that gave me confidence.

No, Lord, I thought. *The spirit of Antichrist may certainly be in this world, but your Spirit is in **me**—and **you** have already overcome the world.*[2]

---

[2] But every spirit that does not acknowledge Jesus is not from God. This is the spirit of the antichrist, which you have heard is coming and even now is already in the world. You, dear children, are from God and have overcome them, because the one who is in you is greater than the one who is in the world. —1 John 4:3-4, NIV

After a few seconds I could make out his features again, could feel him studying me.

"You seem intelligent, Taz, and quite dedicated. I was merely puzzled—no, *intrigued* is a better word—that you seem bent on wasting your time in such . . . fruitless endeavors."

"I think my time is well used. Why would you feel I'm wasting it?"

"Tsk, tsk, Taz. Surely you know that those marked for darkness cannot be, how do you put it? *Redeemed? Saved?*"

The throaty laugh that followed was transfixing, I'll give him that. I shook myself, spoke The Name, and quoted Luke 10:19 under my breath to clear the haze from my mind.[3]

"It ain't over for anyone 'till it's over, Lammie."

"*Lambros*, if you please, Taz. I do demand appropriate respect."

I maybe couldn't *see* his brows pull together in displeasure, but I could sure sense them.

"Sorry, *Lambros*, old chap."

Yikes. Did I just call him old? Well, if the shoe fits . . .

"Sorry . . . again. But, 'marked for darkness'? Every human is marked by sin and, therefore, I suppose you could say, 'marked for darkness.' To my point, however, a person's eternal destination is not *permanently* settled until death occurs. Until death, everyone has the opportunity to choose . . . differently.[4]

---

[3] When the seventy-two disciples returned, they joyfully reported to him, "Lord, even the demons obey us when we use your name!"

"Yes," he told them, "I saw Satan fall from heaven like lightning! Look, I have given you authority over all the power of the enemy, and you can walk among snakes and scorpions and crush them. Nothing will injure you. But don't rejoice because evil spirits obey you; rejoice because your names are registered in heaven."
—Luke 10:17-20, NLT

[4] Just as people are destined to die once, and after that to face judgment, so Christ was sacrificed once to take away the sins of many; and he will appear a second time, not to bear sin, but to bring salvation to those who are waiting for him.
—Hebrews 9:27-28, NIV

"My Lord can—*and will*—snatch many from the jaws of *your* lord before it's all said and done. He is able to save to the uttermost all those who come to him.[5] And those my Lord saves, he sets a seal upon, marking them as *his*."[6]

I gestured in his general vicinity. "But what about you, Lambros? Are you 'marked for darkness'? Are you beyond redemption?"

He guffawed—not in keeping with his elegant manner, either. "But of course. My allegiance has long been settled."

"And yet here you are, talking to *me*, a soldier under the Supreme Commander, because you were—how did you say it? *Intrigued*?"

A flurry of night wisps swirled about him. I would say he was, again, irritated with me.

"Tone, Taz, tone," he chided me. "We've agreed upon a cordial conversation, haven't we? Tossing about allusions to your god's 'über-greatness' is . . . disparaging and off-putting. Not at all tolerant of you."

"Forgive me, Lambros, but I confess that I don't aspire to excel at the PC 'tolerance' game. I just call the facts as I see them."

"What a narrow mind you have," he mocked, drawing himself up.

"Narrow? Yes, but intentionally so. Right and wrong are concrete concepts; they are not relative to the situation, culture, or times. Neither is truth."

"Oh, dear. And how *pedestrian* your views are into the bargain. Certainly, what is 'truth' to one individual is utter nonsense to another. Really, we *must* allow others the . . . er, *grace*, I believe is the word you

---

[5] Therefore He is also able to save to the uttermost those who come to God through Him, since He always lives to make intercession for them. —Hebrews 7:25, NKJV

[6] Now it is God who makes both us and you stand firm in Christ. He anointed us, set his seal of ownership on us, and put his Spirit in our hearts as a deposit, guaranteeing what is to come. —2 Corinthians 1:21-22, NIV

might use? The *grace* to chart their own path to truth." He chuckled at his clever pun.

"Wow. Now I'm confused, Lambros. And I thought you were so, *er, brilliant!* So, you're saying that we should agree that Person A's truth is real and valid and that Person B's truth (which, by the way, totally contradicts Person A's truth) is just as real and just as valid—as long as they are each allowed the freedom to choose their version of truth? Is that it?"

"Taz, don't be pedantic. Of course."

"So truth has nothing to do with reality?"

Lambros hesitated. "Your reality may be different than mine. Your truth may be different, also."

I blew out a breath and shook my head. "I think your concept of reality is a little out of square. Two plus two can only be four. It cannot be five or six or *a breadbox.*

"For example, if I were to pull my Glock 9mm and put it to Person A's head and pull the trigger, the result would be *real.* Gosh! The poor sucker would be *really* dead—not just to himself, but to everyone in the universe, including Person B."

"Shocking," Lambros temporized. "Quite a vulgar illustration."

But then he giggled.

I suppose he couldn't help himself, the thought of all that blood . . .

"Well, I haven't quite completed the illustration. Not only would poor Person A be *really* dead, but if I were to do the same thing to Person B, he would be as equally dead as Person A—in equally the same manner. No difference."

"What is your *point*, dear Taz, because it does elude me," he drawled with biting scorn.

"My point is that *reality* applies equally to all—we do not get to 'choose' our own reality, a reality that is separate from *universal* reality.

"The same physical principles apply equally to all. If you jump off a building, you *will* go splat—I don't care what 'truth' you may espouse."

I folded my arms and waxed to my conclusion. "The physical and spiritual realms may be different, but what happens in the spirit realm is just as real as what happens in the physical realm. Just because spiritual things can't be seen with our eyes—not *yet*, anyway—does not make their consequences any less real—or any less universal. If certain actions make Person A dead spiritually, the same actions will make Person B equally dead spiritually—and Person C, Person D, etc.

"In the same way that actions are universal to all, *truth* is universal to all. Truth, by definition, has only one version, one reality. Person A cannot subscribe to a version of truth that professes to be THE truth without Person B's 'truth' being false. And if only one version of Truth can be true, then all other versions are—*and must be*—false."

"I hadn't taken you for such a nitpicker, Taz." He was waxing incensed—again.

"I'm hardly a nitpicker, Lambros. I'm just a realist. Life is plain, not complex."

"Splicing and dicing words," he mocked.

"The physical life ends at some point—even for you, Lambros. After this physical life ends, eternal life begins. What people choose here, in this life, matters. It matters for all eternity."[7]

A Ω

---

[7] (Jesus speaking) "I tell you the truth, those who listen to my message and believe in God who sent me have eternal life. They will never be condemned for their sins, but they have already passed from death into life." —John 5:24, NLT

CHAPTER 4

HE SEETHED WITH annoyance, over on his chosen side of the fire escape, and I figured we were done. I kept my eyes peeled for his shadowy form to lift off and float away. Maybe even turn into a bat? You know, like in the old movies?

Don't ridicule me. I'd never talked with a vampire before, so what did I know?

I prayed under my breath, wondering what in the world might happen next. Five minutes passed. Ten minutes.

When he didn't leave but I felt his rage had cooled a tad, I cleared my throat. "I'm wondering, Lambros, if you realize that you are not unredeemable."

He snorted—snorted!—and I had to chuckle, so I did. Not at him, but at the situation and at his penchant for the dramatic. The flashing gleam of teeth told me he found *my* humor humorous, just in an odd, *evil* sort of way.

"May I explain?" I asked. I was determined not to waste this unique opportunity. Who knew if such an encounter would ever recur?

The shadowy form bowed—actually *bowed*—his sardonic acquiescence.

Quite the chivalrous and gentlemanly wampyr, aren't you? I laughed inside.

"Thanks, buddy." I licked my lips, praying to the Holy Spirit to give me the right words. "You know . . . when The Lord created the universe, he created only two types of sentient beings—"

"Really, Taz! At least *attempt* to restrain yourself from offending me with that *name*," he protested. "You're not behaving in the spirit of our agreement."

"Really, Lambros!" I retorted (not very charitably), "if The Name *has no power*, what is your problem? If The Name *has* power, why do you defy him?"

He "hrmphed" and his lips curled and drew back from his clamped teeth. My ears caught the minute grinding of long canines against shorter incisors as he gnashed them together.

Way creepy.

"As I was saying," I restrained the unprofitable sarcasm rising in my breast. Just a little. Well, maybe not much.

"As I was saying, *he* created only two types of sentient beings— angels and people. Angels came first and are quite powerful. People came second, but *they*, they were unique in all creation, formed in the image and likeness of *you-very-well-know-who.* [8]

"We people fell into disobedience and that caused the downfall of not just the human race but all creation, including the planet we live on. People should, by rights, be more powerful than angels, because The Book tells us that angels were created to be our servants." [9]

The miasma of darkish air billowed and I could almost feel Lambros swelling in indignation. "You leave *my* kind out entirely," he spat at me. "We are certainly more powerful than mere humans."

"Hogswallop." My tone was a bit more genial. "You are as human as I am. Perverted human, yes, but still human."

"I am *Undead!*" he roared. "Not some lowly, plebian, *person!* I am powerful and immortal!"

"Um, immortal? *Really*? If you're so all-fired immortal, Lammie-pie, let's just chat here until the sun comes up, shall we?"

---

[8] Then God said, "Let us make mankind in our image, in our likeness, so that they may rule over the fish in the sea and the birds in the sky, over the livestock and all the wild animals, and over all the creatures that move along the ground." So God created mankind in his own image, in the image of God he created them; male and female he created them. —Genesis 1:26-27, NIV

[9] Are not all angels ministering spirits sent to serve those who will inherit salvation? Hebrews 1:14, NIV

I pointed to a break between two taller edifices overshadowing my apartment building. "The sun rises right through there, nice and bright, around, oh, say, 6:15 in the morning. Let's just wait here together for the nice, warm, shiny sun, shall we?"

His hazy form jerked in the direction of my pointing finger. It jerked back and he snarled, "So I have one *tiny* vulnerability. What do *you* have, eh, Tazzie-boy? How many ways could I dispatch you? A quick twist of the neck, a little shove from this perch?"

"Look, Lambros," now I was in earnest. "I'm not trying to twist your, er, *tail*. I'm going somewhere, right? Just listen for a sec. okay?"

Again he "hrumphed" and finally, petulantly, muttered, "Fine."

"Thank you," I answered. More than anything, I wanted to get our conversation back on track.

"Look: two forms of intelligent life, angels and people, angels intended to serve people who are made in, er, *his* image. But we people fell from our original state of completeness. At present, we are mere shadows of what we were created to be. After the resurrection, those who belong to *him* will again rise to the original roles God intended for us. And more. Once again the angels will be subject to us."[10]

I paused and then ventured, "So, Lambros, I'm wondering . . . how come . . . how come *your* master, previously of the angelic ranks, so

---

[10] And furthermore, it is not angels who will control the future world we are talking about. For in one place the Scriptures say, "What are mere mortals that you should think about them, or a son of man that you should care for him? Yet you made them only a little lower than the angels and crowned them with glory and honor. You gave them authority over all things." Now when it says "all things," it means nothing is left out. But we have not yet seen all things put under their authority. What we do see is Jesus, who was given a position "a little lower than the angels"; and because he suffered death for us, he is now "crowned with glory and honor." Yes, by God's grace, Jesus tasted death for everyone. —Hebrews 2:5-9, NLT

basically a *fallen* angel,[11] is calling the shots for *you*, a man created in the image and likeness of *you-know-who*?"

"You said it yourself. He's my master." He proclaimed it proudly, I thought, but I wondered—did I detect the ittiest, *bittiest* hint of wariness?

"Yeah, but *why* is he your master? He is, after all, just a fallen angel—a part of the creation—not *The Creator.* Why is he your master, rather than your servant, since that wasn't the original intent?"

I leaned a little in his general direction. "Don't you think, maybe just *a little*, that you may have been, er, compromised? Misled? Suborned? Hoodwinked? Deceived? *Lied to?*"

"My master does not lie," Lambros answered coldly, "especially to *me.*"

I sighed and wiped my hand across my face, weary, but preparing myself for a full-frontal assault. "Lambros, Lambros. Your guy lies to you every time he flaps his lips. Sure, he floats a little truth out there with the lie—gotta make it shiny, gotta make it attractive, after all—but even a little leaven contaminates the whole lump."

"You don't know that! You can't prove that!"

"Lambros, may I remind you what *my* Master said of *your* master?

> *"You belong to your father, **the devil**,*
> *and you want to carry out your father's desires.*
> *He was a murderer from the beginning,*
> *not holding to the truth, for there is no truth in him.*

---

[11] Then war broke out in heaven. Michael and his angels fought against the dragon, and the dragon and his angels fought back. But he was not strong enough, and they lost their place in heaven. The great dragon was hurled down—that ancient serpent called the devil, or Satan, who leads the whole world astray. He was hurled to the earth, and his angels with him. —Revelation 12:7-9, NIV

When he lies, he speaks his native language,
*for **he is a liar and the father of lies**."* [12]

"Consider the source," he hissed.

"I consider *The Source* to be inviolate. He is the beginning and end of all things, and he said, *I am the Way, **the Truth,** and the Life.*[13] He is not a liar—like we men are. Heaven and earth will pass away but not one crossing of a 't' or dotting of an 'i' of what he has said will go unfulfilled."

"*So you say.*" His tone challenged me.

I sighed again. "Look. Lambros, what I'm getting at is this: You've been fed a line of malarkey. The Bible tells us that the god of this age—*your guy*—has blinded the eyes of unbelievers so that they can't see the truth. You have been blinded, too.[14]

"For example: 'The Undead are eternally damned'? and 'The Undead can't be redeemed'? Scripture tells us that Jesus made peace with *everything* in heaven and on earth through his blood on the cross—that tells us that *no one* is beyond redemption.[15] I can show you more."

"Please, Taz, don't discommode yourself," his arch reply floated on the hot, sultry night air.

"But don't you feel used? Manipulated?"

"No more than you likely do." His pat reply was followed by a contemptuous sniff.

---

[12] John 8:44, NIV

[13] Jesus answered, "I am the way and the truth and the life. No one comes to the Father except through me." —John 14:6, NIV

[14] The god of this age has blinded the minds of unbelievers, so that they cannot see the light of the gospel that displays the glory of Christ, who is the image of God. —2 Corinthians 4:4, NIV

[15] For God in all his fullness was pleased to live in Christ, and through him God reconciled everything to himself. He made peace with everything in heaven and on earth by means of Christ's blood on the cross. —Colossians 1:19-20, NLT

I laughed. "No; see, that's one of those half-truths promoted by your master that is actually a lie. First, my allegiance to Jesus—sorry; I realize *The Name* stings—is voluntary.

"Yes, he chose me, but I have to choose him back. It's called 'free will.'[16] Second, the Holy Spirit is a gentleman. If I he asks me to do something (or to not do something) I can choose to obey or not obey. He won't *make* me do his bidding or beat me into submission. I still get to choose. Your guy allow that?"

I posed the provocative question intentionally, of course, and I heard him suck in a breath, ready to retort—only he kinda choked on it or something.

I wasn't sure what was happening; it was like he inhaled to say something and sucked in a bug that flew up his windpipe. He was caught in a coughing fit but at the same time he was backpedaling, floundering, beating the air about himself, trying to back away?

Oh. Yeah. Got it.

I sensed the evil presence, felt the hot breath on my neck, and— automatically, I'm glad to report—I growled, "Demon, I rebuke you in the Name of Jesus!" I tossed the command over my shoulder without looking. "Begone!"[17]

Lambros dropped in a crumpled heap on the fire escape, coughing and hacking, trying to catch his breath. While I had him there, I pressed home with all I had. "Why do you suppose your 'benevolent' master just now dispatched one of his cronies to jerk a knot in your neck, huh?

---

[16] He came to that which was his own, but his own did not receive him. Yet to all who did receive him, to those who believed in his name, he gave the right to become children of God—children born not of natural descent, nor of human decision or a husband's will, but born of God. —John 1:11-13, NIV

[17] Calling the Twelve to him, he began to send them out two by two and gave them authority over impure spirits . . . They drove out many demons and anointed many sick people with oil and healed them. —Mark 6:7 and 13, NIV

"Let me tell you why: *He. Is. Afraid.*

"He is afraid that he will lose you tonight. Oh, he knows the score all right. The Bible says that even the devils believe that there is ONE GOD and they *tremble*.[18]

"They know what is coming! They know they will be judged and that *they **will** bow* before him! Scripture tells us,

> *"For we will all stand before God's judgment seat.*
> *It is written: "As surely as I live," says the Lord,*
> *"every knee will bow before me;*
> *every tongue will acknowledge God.[19]*

"Even Satan and his demons will bow before The Lord on That Day. They are powerless to prevent their own demise[20]—and yet they fight: They fight to delay the inevitable and they fight to take as many souls with them *to hell* as they possibly can—*including yours.*

"As a believer I am not afraid of them, although I recognize that they are evil and have temporary dominion over this fallen world.[21]

"I have schooled myself in God's word so that I recognize demonic forces when I encounter them, and I fight them—not with my own strength, but with the strength of The Lord of Hosts and the Sword of his Powerful, Living Word.

---

[18] You say you have faith, for you believe that there is one God. Good for you! Even the demons believe this, and they tremble in terror. —James 2:19, NLT

[19] Romans 14:10b-11, NIV

[20] . . . God did not spare angels when they sinned, but sent them to hell, putting them in chains of darkness to be held for judgment . . . —2 Peter 2:4, NIV

[21] We know that God's children do not make a practice of sinning, for God's Son holds them securely, and the evil one cannot touch them. We know that we are children of God and that the world around us is under the control of the evil one. And we know that the Son of God has come, and he has given us understanding so that we can know the true God. And now we live in fellowship with the true God because we live in fellowship with his Son, Jesus Christ. He is the only true God, and he is eternal life. —1 John 5:18-20, NLT

"For we are not fighting against flesh-and-blood enemies,
but against evil rulers and authorities of the unseen world,
against mighty powers in this dark world,
and against evil spirits in the heavenly places.[22]

"Listen, Lambros. You sought me out tonight, and not because you are merely 'intrigued.' I believe that you hunger to be released from your bondage. You know your situation is hopeless without Christ. And your master is afraid that you will throw him off and that *Jesus* will set you free into the glorious light of the Children of God."

"That *name*! It burns!" he shrieked, still huddling in the corner.

"His Name does not burn as much as hell will, I assure you! Yes, you are afraid of God—and rightfully so. But you are also afraid of your master—you fear him and what he will do to you," I tell Lambros.

"You fear your master, too," he hissed in response. "In fact, you are *commanded* to fear him!"

"Yes, the Bible commands us to fear God, but it is not the same fear you have for your master. Mine is a reverential awe, an acknowledge-ment that he *is* The Creator and The King of the Universe! I am happy to confess that I am utterly dependent upon him. Scripture tells us plainly,

"Do not be afraid of those who kill the body
but cannot kill the soul.
Rather, be afraid of the One
who can destroy both soul and body in hell."[23]

I waved my finger in the air. "You know what is different between my fear of God and your fear of your master—shall we just say his name?—of *Satan*? My God is honorable and trustworthy! He *loves* me

---

[22] Ephesians 6:12, NLT

[23] Matthew 10:28, NIV

and gave his life for me! Does your master *love you* the way Almighty God loves me?[24]

"See, because he loves me, my hope is in him, the King of Kings and the Lord of Hosts. What hope do you have? I don't fear him when I make a mistake or think my God is waiting to punish me. I don't fear that he is plotting and planning my demise. Why? Because he loved me enough to send his Son to die for me.[25]

"How about you ask yourself this question, Lambros: Why does your master fear this conversation so much that he sends a demon to choke you? No answer? No comment? No clue? Then let me tell you. Satan is afraid you'll figure it out. He's *scared* that you'll realize *he intends to destroy you.*

"Does my God hide his plans from me? No. He has a good purpose for my life here and now and has promised me a resurrected body and eternal life in the glory of his presence. Does your master have anything other than destruction in store for you?"[26]

He dodged my questions. "Resurrection? Bah! It is for the dead. *I* am, as you know, *Undead.*"

A Ω

---

[24] But because of his great love for us, God, who is rich in mercy, made us alive with Christ even when we were dead in transgressions—it is by grace you have been saved. —Ephesians 2:4-5, NIV

[25] You see, at just the right time, when we were still powerless, Christ died for the ungodly. Very rarely will anyone die for a righteous person, though for a good person someone might possibly dare to die. But God demonstrates his own love for us in this: While we were still sinners, Christ died for us. —Romans 5:6-8, NIV

[26] (Jesus speaking) "I am the gate; whoever enters through me will be saved. They will come in and go out, and find pasture. The thief comes only to steal and kill and destroy; I have come that they may have life, and have it to the full. I am the good shepherd. The good shepherd lays down his life for the sheep." —John 10:9-11, NIV

CHAPTER 5

"FOR THE UNDEAD it is already too late," Lambros coughed. He pulled himself into a tidy, inky heap in the corner of the fire escape. "I am damned for all eternity."

He seemed resigned to his fate.

"You believe all that vampire lore?"

"Of course. Why wouldn't I?" he pulled himself up and leaned into the shadows, becoming one with them again. "Would Wikipedia lie? Would Hollywood? What they say is true."

Wikipedia?

I shook my astounded head. "Sooooo everything online is true? I suppose you also believe that the Professor from Gilligan's Island is really the Zodiac Killer? Sheesh."

"Taz, you mean well, I'm sure," he muttered, almost managing to sound dejected, "but we *Nosferatu* are neither alive nor dead; we don't get to play by the same rules as people. There's no 'happily ever after' for us."

"Well, I know you believe all the myths about vampires, Lambros, but believing in something doesn't necessarily make it so. I can believe I'm a leprechaun all I want, but it will never make me one.

"Yes; I agree that you are damned at present; however, the *real* question should be, is your judgment without remedy?

"Reality is concrete and universal, remember? It can be only *one thing* and one thing *only* for *everyone*. Either vampire lore is truth and God's Word is a lie—or God's Word is truth and vampire lore is a lie. One of them is right, which means the other is *wrong*—utterly wrong.

"Why don't you let me show you?" I implored.

He seemed to have recovered somewhat from the demon's chokehold. It was now time to loose him from The Devil's stronghold.

"Let's talk about regeneration," I began. "You have a dead, non-beating heart, yes?"

The pile of shadows nodded. "As I said, dear boy, we are The Undead." His despair was palpable, but he clung to his bravado.

"Have you never heard what Ezekiel the Prophet wrote?

> *"A new heart also will I give you,*
> *and a new spirit will I put within you:*
> *and I will take away the stony heart out of your flesh,*
> *and I will give you **a heart of flesh**.[27]*

"Sounds custom-made for your, er, circumstance, doesn't it?" I asked. "Scripture also says,

> *"But after that the kindness and love*
> *of God our Saviour toward man appeared,*
> *not by works of righteousness which we have done,*
> *but according to his mercy he saved us,*
> *by the washing of **regeneration**,*
> *and renewing of the Holy Ghost[28]*

"To regenerate means to *make alive that which was dead*. You, Lambros, aren't *dead*, per se, but, then again, you aren't exactly *alive* either. It doesn't matter to God—he can make alive whomever he wills, be they dead or merely 'Undead'—he has authority over all spiritual matters."[29]

"You make light of our condition!" Lambros growled. "And you are twisting your own master's words."

---

[27] Ezekiel 36:26, KJV

[28] Titus 3:4-5, KJV

[29] You were dead because of your sins and because your sinful nature was not yet cut away. Then God made you alive with Christ, for he forgave all our sins. He canceled the record of the charges against us and took it away by nailing it to the cross. In this way, he disarmed the spiritual rulers and authorities. He shamed them publicly by his victory over them on the cross. —Colossians 2:13-15, NLT

"Hardly. Every person born into the world is born with a fallen nature. We are *all* Undead—or *The Walking Dead* if you prefer.[30]

"All of us are living in doomed bodies—bodies that are already corrupting and are subject to death.[31] Our dying bodies are inhabited by spiritually dead hearts—dead in trespasses and sin, destined to be separated from God for all eternity. How is that any different than you?"

"But surely it is a reference or a metaphor that applies only to spiritual regeneration!"

"Why can't it be both?" I queried. "Is anything impossible with Almighty God?"[32]

We were down to it, so I pressed him. Pressed hard. "If anyone—*anyone*—is in Christ, he becomes a new creation, *a new creature.* Everything old passes away because the resurrection power of Jesus makes us new. He severs us from the past and gives us a new beginning.[33]

He growled again, determined to maintain his position

"Listen, Lambros. To those who surrender to the Lordship of Jesus, God the Father promises that the Holy Spirit of God himself will dwell in us.[34]

---

[30] As for you, you were dead in your transgressions and sins, in which you used to live when you followed the ways of this world and of the ruler of the kingdom of the air, the spirit who is now at work in those who are disobedient. All of us also lived among them at one time, gratifying the cravings of our flesh and following its desires and thoughts. Like the rest, we were by nature deserving of wrath. —Ephesians 2:1-3, NIV

[31] But if Christ is in you, then even though your body is subject to death because of sin, the Spirit gives life because of righteousness. —Romans 8:10, NIV

[32] Jesus looked at them and said, "With man this is impossible, but with God all things are possible." —Matthew 19:26, NIV

[33] So then, if anyone is in Christ, he is a new creation; what is old has passed away—look, what is new has come! —2 Corinthians 5:17, NET

[34] Don't you realize that your body is the temple of the Holy Spirit, who lives in you and was given to you by God? You do not belong to yourself, for God bought you with a high price. So you must honor God with your body. —1 Corinthians 6:19-20, NLT

"And he further says,

> *"And if the Spirit of him who*
> *raised Jesus from the dead is living in you,*
> ***he who raised Christ from the dead***
> ***will also give life to your mortal bodies***
> *because of his Spirit who lives in you.*[35]

"The Bible declares that the Holy Spirit is a *life-giving Spirit.*[36] He has the power to make your Undead vampire body *alive*, Lambros— either *now* or later at the resurrection when all who are *in Christ* will rise![37]

I took a chance. I walked toward Lambros and extended my hand. "The Savior is waiting to receive you, Lambros. So, will you bow your knee to Jesus now? Or will you bow to him at the judgment when it is too late?"

He shuddered and turned his shadowed face farther into the darkness.

A Ω

---

[35] Romans 8:11, NIV

[36] So now there is no condemnation for those who belong to Christ Jesus. And because you belong to him, the power of the life-giving Spirit has freed you from the power of sin that leads to death. —Romans 8:1-2, NLT

[37] For the Lord himself will come down from heaven, with a loud command, with the voice of the archangel and with the trumpet call of God, and the dead in Christ will rise first. After that, we who are still alive and are left will be caught up together with them in the clouds to meet the Lord in the air. And so we will be with the Lord forever. —1 Thessalonians 4:16-17, NIV

CHAPTER 6

"I HAVE DONE MANY things . . . things my master lauds and rewards. Things that cannot be undone." He sneered his words in the scornful, disdaining tone of the thoroughly debauched, those whose consciences are seared and unfeeling.

"Name them," I challenged him. "I dare you."

His nostrils flared. "You think I am ashamed? You think I regret my deeds? I proclaim them with pride!

"Over the centuries I have corrupted many young women . . . and a few young men . . . seducing them and stealing their virtue—feasting on their flesh before feasting on their blood! And some I have condemned to eternal damnation by making them drink of *my* blood before draining them.[38]

"These things I have done because it is my nature to do them," he added. "I have made offspring in *my* image and likeness and they have, in turn, recruited select others to join our ranks." He was boasting, but everything in his boast was weak. Regret lurked behind his proud words.

Perhaps his conscience was not completely seared, completely calloused?

"I don't believe you, Lambros. If you do not regret your deeds, then why are you here talking to me?" I demanded. "I believe that you are, deep down, ashamed. I believe you do regret your deeds—and I believe you regret the futility of your life. I believe you are desperate."

"You know *nothing*," he retorted.

---

[38] Or do you not know that wrongdoers will not inherit the kingdom of God? Do not be deceived: Neither the sexually immoral nor idolaters nor adulterers nor men who have sex with men nor thieves nor the greedy nor drunkards nor slanderers nor swindlers will inherit the kingdom of God. And that is what some of you were. But you were washed, you were sanctified, you were justified in the name of the Lord Jesus Christ and by the Spirit of our God. —1 Corinthians 6:9-11, NIV

"I know nothing? Let me tell you what I know," I responded in kind. "I know that you are *still a man*, like me. I know that you are dead in your sins—*just as I was*. And *just as I was*, you are not so all-fired 'special' that you are beyond the reach of God's redeeming power!

"*Jesus* said—oh, do stop flinching, Lambros! You will hear The Name through eternity so you'd better get used to it—*Jesus* said,

> *"For God so loved the world*
> *that he gave his one and only Son,*
> *that **whoever** believes in him*
> *shall not perish but have eternal life.*[39]

"The word *whoever* is the Greek word *pas*. You *are* familiar with Greek, my *brilliant* friend, right? You already know the Greek word *pas* means *each, every, any, all,* and *everyone*. It *includes* everyone and *excludes* no one. Anyone can believe on Jesus and have eternal life— even you."

"Not so," Lambros retorted. "You forget I am not like you. You say I am a man like you, but you would be wrong. You are created in *your* master's image and likeness," he snarled. "Well, I am created in *my* master's image and likeness. Nothing can or will ever undo that. I am my master's offspring and I will share his glory for all eternity."

"You will share his eternal *glory*? You cannot be serious! Your master has already been judged[40] and his eternal fate assigned to him. That fate will not be glorious—it will be *eternal torment*. Jesus himself said Satan will be thrown into the eternal fires.

---

[39] John 3:16, NIV

[40] (Jesus speaking) "And when he [the Holy Spirit] comes, he will convict the world of its sin, and of God's righteousness, and of the coming judgment. The world's sin is that it refuses to believe in me. Righteousness is available because I go to the Father, and you will see me no more. Judgment will come because the ruler [prince] of this world has already been judged." —John 16:8-11, NLT

"Those of Satan's kingdom will share in the torment of that eternal fire—*you* will share the torment of that eternal fire unless you surrender your soul to The Savior."[41]

"You are merely parsing words, Taz. In the end your words make no difference."

I ignored his barbs. "Your master can only *destroy*. Only Jesus can give you eternal life. *Eternal life*, Lambros! Not eternal death! He wants to rescue you from the kingdom of darkness and bring you into his kingdom of light.[42] Jesus died to extend this offer to you: *Exchange your eternal damnation for eternal life.*"

"No!" His objection was fierce, but it was in disbelief. "This *cannot* be so."

"It is exactly so! You are here, talking to me, because you sense that time running out for yourself, Lambros, and you have become desperate. Oh, you are sorry for the things you have done—not because they are *wrong* but because you fear their consequences. This is not godly sorrow but the sorrow of the world. Godly sorrow leads *away* from sin and *toward* God.[43]

"But there is a day coming, a day the Bible calls the day of God's wrath."

---

[41] (Jesus speaking) "Then he will say to those on his left, 'Depart from me, you who are cursed, into the eternal fire prepared for the devil and his angels."
—Matthew 25:41, NIV

[42] For he has rescued us from the kingdom of darkness and transferred us into the Kingdom of his dear Son, who purchased our freedom and forgave our sins.
—Colossians 1:13-14, NLT

[43] For the kind of sorrow God wants us to experience leads us away from sin and results in salvation. There's no regret for that kind of sorrow. But worldly sorrow, which lacks repentance, results in spiritual death. Just see what this godly sorrow produced in you! Such earnestness, such concern to clear yourselves, such indignation, such alarm, such longing to see me, such zeal, and such a readiness to punish wrong. You showed that you have done everything necessary to make things right.
—2 Corinthians 7:10-11, NLT

"On That Day[44] he will demand an accounting of all humankind. Those who have confessed their wrongs and turned away from them, turning to Jesus for undeserved mercy, need not fear that day. But those who hold to their evil actions and refuse the gift of God (his Son, Jesus) will experience great regret!

"Does The Lord *want* you to suffer the consequences of your sins? No, but sin has a penalty that must be paid, and that penalty is death. *Someone must die to pay for your sin!*[45]

"So what did The Lord do? Did he leave us without hope to die for our own sins? *No.* He asked his own Son to pay for your sins, Lambros. *His own Son.* In the greatest act of love the world has ever seen, The Lord asked his Son to die for you. For me. For humanity.

"And his Son said, *Yes. I will.*

> *"For God did not send his Son into the world*
> *to condemn the world,*
> *but to save the world **through him**.*[46]

---

[44] So when you, a mere human being, pass judgment on them and yet do the same things, do you think you will escape God's judgment? Or do you show contempt for the riches of his kindness, forbearance and patience, not realizing that God's kindness is intended to lead you to repentance? But because of your stubbornness and your unrepentant heart, you are storing up wrath against yourself for the day of God's wrath, when his righteous judgment will be revealed. —Romans 2:3-5, NIV

[45] For everyone has sinned; we all fall short of God's glorious standard. Yet God freely and graciously declares that we are righteous. He did this through Christ Jesus when he freed us from the penalty for our sins. For God presented Jesus as the sacrifice for sin. People are made right with God when they believe that Jesus sacrificed his life, shedding his blood. This sacrifice shows that God was being fair when he held back and did not punish those who sinned in times past, for he was looking ahead and including them in what he would do in this present time. God did this to demonstrate his righteousness, for he himself is fair and just, and he declares sinners to be right in his sight when they believe in Jesus. — Romans 3:23-26, NLT

[46] John 3:17, NIV

"The Lord God has made a way for us to escape the coming wrath: Repent of your evil doings—that is, turn from them *in sincerity*—receive the sacrifice of Jesus' life on the cross as payment for your sins, and surrender to his lordship over your life."[47]

"How can I do that?" Lambros spoke aloud but he was, I think, asking himself that question.

"How dare you not?" I answered him. "On that day, the day of wrath, each of your sins will be set before you, exposed for the world to see. You will have no excuse when you stand before God. Even worse, he will ask you what you have done with his Son, *the Son he sent to die for you* in order to save you.

"Scripture tells us that no one can come to Jesus unless the Father draws him. The Father is drawing you—calling you!—right now. That is why you felt compelled to follow me tonight.[48]

"Even right now, the passages of God's Living Word that I have spoken to you are working in you, working in your soul to expose its thoughts and intents and to convince you of the truth—all to draw you to the Lordship of Christ:

"For the word of God is alive and powerful.
It is sharper than the sharpest two-edged sword,
cutting between soul and spirit, between joint and marrow.

---

[47] "Whoever believes in him is not condemned, but whoever does not believe stands condemned already because they have not believed in the name of God's one and only Son. This is the verdict: Light has come into the world, but people loved darkness instead of light because their deeds were evil. Everyone who does evil hates the light, and will not come into the light for fear that their deeds will be exposed. But whoever lives by the truth comes into the light, so that it may be seen plainly that what they have done has been done in the sight of God." —John 3:18-21, NIV

[48] (Jesus speaking) "For no one can come to me unless the Father who sent me draws them to me, and at the last day I will raise them up. As it is written in the Scriptures, 'They will all be taught by God.' Everyone who listens to the Father and learns from him comes to me." —John 6:44-45, NLT

It exposes our innermost thoughts and desires.
Nothing in all creation is hidden from God.
Everything is naked and exposed before his eyes,
*and he is the **one** to whom we are accountable.*[49]

"So what will you tell The Lord God Almighty on that day, Lambros? *How will you explain that you rejected the very Son of God?*

He was silent but I could see his silhouette, clothed with smoky darkness, *shaking,* as though he were being pulled apart, being torn asunder. And I knew that he was. A great battle was raging within him— the spirits of darkness battling the convincing power of the Holy Spirit of God for the soul of this one, depraved, Undead man.

"Today you have heard the Gospel, the Good News," I said softly. "Now you must choose whom you will serve."

I could tell the Holy Spirit was moving him, wooing him.

"But I don't deserve . . . mercy." His whisper floated toward me on the night.

"No one—not one of us—does. It is a picture of how good The Lord is that he paid the price for our sin. We don't deserve mercy, but he gives it anyway. Because he loves us."

Unexpected lightning sizzled and crackled around us. A thunderous boom ripped the stillness of the summer night, rocking our fragile perch high above the street.

My *spidey-sense* freaked out.

Uh-oh.

Playtime was over.

A Ω

---

[49] Hebrews 4:12-13, NLT

CHAPTER 7

LAMBROS' CHIN LIFTED, his nostrils flaring and sniffing. He shivered and his eyes blazed scarlet and darted about.

"They are coming for you," I whispered.

"Can you protect me from them . . . from *him*?" It was a mark of how deeply his desperation ran that he would beg *me* to shield him.

I swallowed. "Temporarily, perhaps," I answered, "but you cannot lean on me for long. Your only sure hope is in Jesus himself—only he can save you from your just punishment. Now is the time to make your decision. God has clearly told us, *I have set before you life and death, blessings and curses. Now choose life, so that you and your children may live!*"[50]

Excuse me if my voice rose in pitch and volume—I was shouting—but the very air was charged with sinister foreboding. It was time for Lambros to make his move. I did not want to think about his fate should he delay longer and, I confess that, even with all my combat experience, I was shaking so hard, my knees were knocking together.

The wind gusted and pitched and on it rode . . . a terrible force. A malevolent being.

"Jesus," I murmured. "Jesus." The sense of The Lord's presence and power filled and comforted me, but over in his corner Lambros was alone, exposed and defenseless.

In a show of bravado, he stretched to his full and impressive height and width. He raised his arms and grew taller still! I could see he was gripped with fear and his terror served to unmask him. For the first time I saw him clearly: His features were young and lean, cut and hawkish; his lips red and cruel.

Oh, but his eyes! His eyes passed over me and I glimpsed the aged spirit within—the cunning, sin-wizened soul that inhabited what was only a youthful façade. He was a creature of decadence and moral decay.

---

[50] Deuteronomy 30:19, NIV

I grieved for his fate! I mourned over the payment that would be demanded this night. "Lambros!"

The wind was keening about our heads now, catching away my shouted warning. The evil that gusted on that wind was like nothing I'd experienced. The malevolent force grew in magnitude and intensity; with it descended a smoking stench that enveloped us.

I felt no fear for myself—I am, after all, one of the redeemed of The Lord. Satan has no legal footing in my life.

The Holy Spirit of The Lord God rose up in me. "Lambros! Call upon The Name! Call upon *Jesus* to save you!"

Out of the smoking cloud something reached for Lambros—a grotesque hand that slipped through the black and foul mist to grasp him. Talons compassed Lambros chest, tearing into his body. Before my eyes the curled claws, misshapen and cruel, squeezed and crushed him.

"Jesus! Jesus!" I screamed, but the evil wind carried away my words.

I felt the world shudder: Under my feet the fire escape swayed and the building trembled as though the earth were quaking. It was! A roar filled my head. I could not stand and was rocked to my knees. I heard and saw the bolts that cemented the fire escape to the building groaning, grinding, and wrenching free. The iron of our fragile perch screed and twisted away from the brick walls.

Lambros' face turned toward me, contorted with agony. He would perish before the fire escape dragged us to the streets below—I could see that. As "immortal" as Lambros believed himself to be, his master would soon destroy The Undead body in which Lambros dwelled and carry his soul to hell.

Again I urged him. "Lambros! Surrender to the Lordship of Christ!"

I saw his lips move. Blood dribbled from them, but I saw his lips move.

I saw his lips move . . . forming the word *Jesus*.

In hindsight . . . I can only write what I *felt* rather than what I *saw* in that moment. It was . . .

Explosive. Instantaneous. Supernatural.

A truly awful screech of fury rent the air. Lambros crashed onto the fire escape—and between him and the clawed fist stood a great, sword-wielding presence.

I could scarcely look at the creature for the radiance of his form. His face was set in hard, righteous lines and he swung his sword overhead as though the iron framework of the fire escape did not exist—and it might as well not have, for the angelic being stood *above* the iron platform, not on it, and moved where he wished without hindrance.

"Mine!" an outraged voice bellowed.

"He has called upon The Name," the angel responded. "**It is written**: *Everyone who calls upon the name of The Lord will be saved.*[51] **It is also written:** *The Lord will set his seal of ownership on him!*"[52]

Shrieks of rage and denial followed and the stinking cloud swelled with ominous energy. In response, the angel swung his sword in a flaming, protecting arc over Lambros.

The angel's voice was like a trumpet, clear and strong and piercing. "You can no longer claim this soul. He has been bought with The Price!"

I tore my eyes from the scene before me and fastened them on Lambros. His bleeding body lay in a twisted, unnatural position a few feet from me. All shadows had fled and clear, pure light illuminated him. Nothing remained veiled or hidden.

And yet, a shimmering, white disk—brighter still—hovered over and came to rest upon his head.

The Seal of The Lord!

---

[51] Romans 10:13, NIV

[52] Now it is God who makes both us and you stand firm in Christ. He anointed us, set his seal of ownership on us, and put his Spirit in our hearts as a deposit, guaranteeing what is to come. 2 Corinthians 1:21-22, NIV

The seal melted and flowed over Lambros, beginning at the top of his head then spreading downward over his entire body. The flowing ointment brightened until a sheen of glory encompassed him.

"Oh, Lord God! Oh, Lord God!" I cried. "Holy! Holy! Holy! You are worthy to be praised!"

The splendor of the risen King and Savior was upon us and all else faded. The howling wind quieted and the evil presence with its foul odor slinked off into the night.

Peaceful calm descended, and the Glory of God reigned around us.

I looked again to Lambros. The angel knelt beside him and lifted him into a sitting position.

In awe I watched . . . the years return to him, drawing down his youth, restoring his true body, full of age, until only a very, *very* old man remained.

With some difficulty he raised his eyes—eyes filled with tearful, joyous wonder. They found mine.

"Thank you," he whispered.

The angel touched him once more. Where an aged Lambros had been, a skiff of dust held his shape and then collapsed and dispersed in the night breeze.

He was gone.

I fastened my gaze on the angel, asking a silent question.

"He is with The Lord now, friend."

The corners of his mouth turned upward. "His repentance and redemption this night tore a great hole in the dark kingdom," the Messenger proclaimed. His smile widened and with his chin he gestured toward me.

"Well done, Taz."

Α Ω

CHAPTER 8

I AWOKE IN PRETTY much the same position as I'd fallen, exhausted, into my bed. The events of last evening came flooding back into my consciousness.

I thought I would be fatigued mentally and physically, but as I stretched I found that I was, *curiously*, refreshed.

It was already late in the morning and the sun spilled through my lone window. *It's all right,* I thought. *I won't be haunting the day-labor lines today. I have a more pressing task.*

I would record the events of last night while they were still fresh in my mind. I sat down to my laptop and opened a new file, Jesus' words to his disciples ringing in my mind:

> *Behold, I send you forth as sheep*
> *in the midst of wolves:*
> *be ye therefore wise as serpents,*
> *and harmless as doves.* [53]

Before I could begin, someone was pounding on my door. I opened it and looked into the hallway. My apartment's maintenance man was taping a notice to the door of my neighbor's apartment across the corridor. A notice already hung on my door.

"What's up?"

He turned. "Had us a major quake last night, that's what. Whole building shook pretty good. Weren't you here? Didn't you feel it?"

"Yeah; I felt it."

A big ten-four on that.

"Well, the city's gonna be inspecting the building this week for structural damage, but we already know the quake loosened some of the fire escapes."

---

[53] Matthew 10:16, KJV

He scowled at me. "Don't be hangin' out on yours until we get them checked out, hear? They ain't safe." He sauntered down the hall, pounded on another door, and taped a notice to it.

"Roger that," I whispered.

I went back inside and sat down in front of my laptop again.

How would I capture what had happened? Where to begin?

Oh.

Oh, yeah.

I began to pound the keyboard . . .

My spidey-sense leapt into high alert. We were down in The Glades passing out little books about Jesus . . .

A Ω

The End

About the Author

VIKKI KESTELL'S PASSION for people and their stories is evident in her readers' affection for her characters and unusual plotlines. Two often-repeated sentiments are, "I feel like I know these people," and, "I'm right there, in the book, experiencing what the characters experience."

Vikki holds a Ph.D. in Organizational Learning and Instructional Technologies. She left a career of twenty-plus years in government, academia, and corporate life to pursue writing full time. "Writing is the best job ever," she admits, "and the most demanding."

Also an accomplished speaker and teacher, Vikki and her husband Conrad Smith make their home in Albuquerque, New Mexico.

To keep abreast of new book releases, sign up for Vikki's newsletter on her website, **http://www.vikkikestell.com**, find her on Facebook at **http://www.facebook.com/vikki.kestell**, or follow her on BookBub, **https://www.bookbub.com/authors/vikki-kestell**.

www.faith-filledfiction.com | www.vikkikestell.com

www.ingramcontent.com/pod-product-compliance
Lightning Source LLC
Chambersburg PA
CBHW060421310726
48976CB00003B/1139